A small man stood in the center of the room. He was gray and unwrinkled. He smiled courteously.

"I am Governor-General Mellis," he said. "You must be Mr. Ewing from Corwin. Won't you please come in?"

Ewing stepped into the room. "I'll make my visit brief, he said. "I'm here to ask for Earth's help to defeat the coming Klodni invasion." Quickly he sketched out an account of what had been happening, adding, "And we did send several messages to Earth. But they must have gone astray en route. So I have come in person."

Mellis moved about the room in impatient birdlike strutting motions before replying. "The messages did not go astray. We did not answer them because there is no possible way we can help you, Mr. Ewing."

"I don't understand."

"We have no weapons, no military forces, no spaceships, and, most importantly, no ability or desire to fight."

A chill crept over Ewing. He had crossed fifty light-years of space— for nothing.

STEPSONS OF TERRA

by
ROBERT SILVERBERG

ace books
A Division of Charter Communications Inc.
A GROSSET & DUNLAP COMPANY
1120 Avenue of the Americas
New York, New York 10036

STEPSONS OF TERRA

Copyright ©, 1958, by Ace Books, Inc.

An ACE Book

Printed in U.S.A.

TO RANDALL GARRETT

STEPSONS OF TERRA

Introduction

Unless I have lost count, which is entirely possible, STEPSONS OF TERRA was my sixth novel—which makes it a very early work even among my early work, because in the far-off days of the 1950's I was writing a novel every few months, and I had a couple of dozen of the things on my record before I sprouted my first gray hair.

Beyond any doubt my first book was the juvenile novel, REVOLT ON ALPHA C, which I wrote in 1954 when I was still practically a juvenile myself. Then came another juvenile, STARMAN'S QUEST, in 1956, and later that year my first ostensibly adult novel, THE THIRTEENTH IMMORTAL and in early 1957 the quite respectable novel MASTER OF LIFE AND DEATH—which probably ought to be given another turn in print one of these days. A few months later I wrote INVADERS FROM EARTH, another early book that causes me no embarrassment today. That's five, and so STEPSONS OF TERRA, written in October of 1957, would be the sixth. Of course, there were also the two "Robert Randall" collaborations with Randall Garrett, THE SHROUDED PLANET and THE DAWNING OF LIGHT, in 1955 and 1956, but those weren't solo jobs. And there were a couple of items like the pseudonymous LEST WE FORGET THEE, O EARTH (1957) and INVISIBLE BARRIERS (1957) that were patched together out of previously published magazine pieces, but they weren't originally conceived as full-length novels, and I don't feel like counting them, and I hope you'll be willing to ignore them too. So the book you are now holding is my sixth novel, give or take a few exceptions and footnotes.

It was written at the behest of Larry T. Shaw, a bespectacled and pipesmoking gentleman who edited a pair of magazines called *Infinity* and *Science Fiction Adventures*. Shaw, an old-time s-f fan, might have had a splendid career as an editor if he had ever found a major publisher to back him, for his taste was superb and he had the useful knack of coaxing writers to do their best work without seeming actually to be nagging them; but it was his fate always to work for marginal companies in short-lived ventures. (He has moved to California, like almost everyone else I knew in New York in those days, and edits a line of paperbacks out of Los Angeles for a company you've probably never heard of.) *Infinity* was his special pride, a low-budget magazine that ran high-budget stories by the likes of Arthur C. Clarke, Isaac Asimov, James Blish, Damon Knight, C.M. Kornbluth, and Algis Budrys; it even published Harlan Ellison's first science fiction story. I was a regular contributor to *Infinity* and many of my best short stories appeared there. The companion magazine, *Science Fiction Adventures,* was less ambitious, a blood-and-thunder operation done strictly for fun, featuring novelets of interstellar intrigue and blazing ray-guns. I was a regular contributor to SFA, too: in fact, I practically wrote the whole magazine. As I look through my file copies, I see a long story or two by me (usually under some pseudonym) in virtually every issue—"Battle for the Thousand Suns," "Slaves of the Star Giants," "Spawn of the Deadly Sea," and so on. I had fun writing these melodramas of the spaceways, and the readers evidently enjoyed them too, for my stories (under whatever pseudonym) were usually the most popular offerings in each issue.

The original format of SFA provided Three Complete

New Action Novels" (actually, novelets 15,000 to 20,000 words in length) in each issue, plus a few short stories and features. But with the seventh issue, October, 1957, editor Shaw decided to vary the pattern a bit, running only two "novels," a long one and a short one. I was his most reliable contributor, so he asked me to write the "Book-Length Novel" to lead off that issue. I turned in a 28,000-word piece called "Thunder Over Starhaven," which appeared under a pseudonym and which I eventually expanded into a novel. The innovation was successful, apparently, for soon Shaw tried another experiment: filling virtually an entire issue with *one* novel.

Again he asked me to do the job. This time it was agreed that the story would appear under my own byline, since "Robert Silverberg" was by now a better known name than any of the pseudonyms I had been using in the magazine; and, since the story would bear my own name, I was a trifle less flamboyant about making use of the pulp-magazine clichés beloved by the magazine's readers. There would be no hissing villains and basilisk-eyed princesses in this one, no desperate duels with dagger and mace, no feudal overlords swaggering about the stars. Rather, I would write a straightforward science fiction novel, strongly plotted but not unduly weighted toward breathless adventure.

"Shadow on the Stars" is what I called it, and that was the name it appeared under in the April, 1958 issue of *Science Fiction Adventures*. The cover announced in big yellow letters, "A COMPLETE NEW BOOK— 35¢" and indeed it did take up most of the issue, spanning 112 of the 130 pages and leaving room only for two tiny short stories and the feature columns. Mainly it was a time-paradox novel—a theme that always has fascinated me—but there was at least one concession to the traditional policy of the magazine, a vast space battle involving an "unstoppable armada" of "seven hundred seventy-five dreadnaughts." I chose to handle the big battle scene, though, in a very untraditional underplayed manner, as you will see; and I did a bit of fooling around with the ending, too, providing *two* twentieth chapters.

The readers loved it. The next issue was full of letters of praise, including one that said, "Silverberg is becoming a really disciplined artist," and asserted that "Shadow on the Stars" seemed somehow to synthesize the previously antithetical traditions of Robert A. Heinlein and E.E. Smith. (Actually, I thought it owed more to A.E. van Vogt.) And then *Science Fiction Adventures* went out of business, for reasons unconnected with the quantity of material I was contributing to it. A *lot* of magazines folded in 1958, including a few that I never wrote for at all.

The next destination for "Shadow on the Stars" was Ace Books. Editor Donald A. Wollheim bought it, retitled it STEPSONS OF TERRA, and published it later in 1958 in his Ace Double Novel series, with a book by a British writer, Lan Wright, on the other side.

What Lan Wright is doing these days, I have no idea. But here is STEPSONS OF TERRA, back in print for the first time since its historic original appearance eighteen or nineteen years ago, for your amusement.

Robert Silverberg
Oakland, California
April 1976

ONE

EWING woke slowly, sensing the coldness all about him. It was slowly withdrawing down the length of his body; his head and shoulders were out of the freeze now, the rest of his body gradually emerging. He stirred as well as he could, and the delicately spun web of foam that had cradled him in the journey across space shivered as he moved.

He extended a hand and heaved downward on the lever six inches from his wrist. A burst of fluid shot forward from the spinnerettes above him, dissolving the web that bound him. The coldness drained from his legs. Stiffly he rose, moving as if he were very old, and stretched gingerly.

He had slept eleven months, fourteen days, and some six hours, according to the panel above his sleeping area. The panel registered time in Galactic Absolute Units. And the second, the Galactic Absolute Unit of temporal measure, was an arbitrary figure, accepted by the galaxy only because it had been devised by the mother world.

Ewing touched an enameled stud and a segment of the inner surface of the ship's wall swung away, revealing a soft glowing vision-plate. A planet hung centered in the green depths of the plate—a planet green itself, with vast seas bordering its continents.

Earth.

Ewing knew what his next task was. Moving quickly, now that circulation was returning to his thawed limbs, he strode to the compact bulk of the subetheric generator on the opposite wall and spun the contact dial. A blue light glowed.

"Baird Ewing speaking," he said to the pickup grid. "I wish to report that I've taken up a position in orbit around Earth after a successful flight. All's well so far. I'll be descending to Earth shortly. Further reports will follow."

He broke contact. This very moment, he knew, his words were leaping across the galaxy toward his home world, via subetheric carrier wave. Fifteen days would elapse before his message arrived on Corwin.

Ewing had wanted to stay awake, all the long months of his solitary trip. There was reading he wanted to do, and music disks to play. The idea of spending nearly a year asleep was appalling to him; all that time wasted!

But they had been adamant. "You're crossing sixteen parsecs of space in a one-man ship," they told him. "Nobody can stay awake all that time and come out of it sane, Ewing. And we need you sane."

He tried to protest. It was no good. The people of Corwin were sending him to Earth at great expense to do a job of vital importance; unless they could be

2

absolutely certain that he would arrive in good condition, they would do better sending someone else. Reluctantly, Ewing yielded. They lowered him into the nutrient bath and showed him how to trip the foot levers that brought about suspension and the hand levers that would release him when his time was up. They sealed off his ship and shot it into the dark, a lonely raft on the broad sea, a coffin-sized spaceship built for one. . . .

At least ten minutes went by before he was fully restored to normal physiological functioning. He stared in the mirror at the strange silken stubble that had sprouted on his face. He looked oddly emaciated; he had never been a fleshy man, but now he looked skeletonic, his cheeks shrunken, his skin tight-drawn over the jutting bones of his face. His hair seemed to have faded too; it had been a rich auburn on that day in 3805 when he left Corwin on his emergency mission to Earth, but now it was a dark, nondescript mud-brown. Ewing was a big man, long-muscled rather than stocky, with a fierce expression contradicted by mild, questioning eyes.

His stomach felt hollow. His shanks were spindly. He felt drained of vigor.

But there was a job to do.

Adjoining the subetheric generator was an in-system communicator. He switched it on, staring at the pale ball that was Earth in the screen on the far wall. A crackle of static rewarded him. He held his breath, waiting, waiting for the first words he would have heard in pure Terrestrial. He wondered if they would understand his Anglo-Corwin.

After all, it was nearly a thousand years since the colony had been planted, and almost five hundred since the people of Corwin had last had intercourse of any kind with Earth. Languages diverge, in five hundred years.

A voice said, "Earth station Double Prime. Who calls, please? Speak up. Speak, please."

Ewing smiled. It was intelligible!

He said, "One-man ship out of the Free World of Corwin calling. I'm a stabilized orbit fifty thousand kilometers above Earth ground level. Request permission to land at coordinates of your designation."

There was a long silence, too long to be attributed sheerly to transmission lag. Ewing wondered if he had spoken too quickly, or if his words had lost their Terrestrial meanings.

Finally came a response: "Free World of *which*, did you say?"

"Corwin. Epsilon Ursae Majoris XII. It's a former Terrestrial colony."

Again there was an uncomfortable pause. "Corwin. . .Corwin. Oh. I guess it's okay for you to land. You have a warp-drive ship?"

"Yes," Ewing said. "With photonic modifiers, of course. And ion-beam for atmospheric passage."

His Earthside respondent said, "Are photonic modifiers radioactive?"

Ewing was taken aback for a moment. Frowning at the speaker grid, he said, "If you mean radioactive in the normal sense of emitting hard particles, no. The photonic modifier merely converts—" He stopped. "Do I have to explain the whole thing to you?"

"Not unless you want to stay up there all day,

4

Corwin. If your ship's not hot, come on down. Coördinates for landing will follow.''

Ewing carefully jotted the figures down as they came in, read them back for confirmation, thanked the Earthman, and signed off. He integrated the figures and programmed them for the ship's calculators.

His throat felt dry. Something about the Earthman's tone of voice troubled him. The man had been too flip, careless of mind, impatient.

Perhaps I was expecting too much, Ewing thought. *After all, he was just doing a routine job.*

It was a jarring beginning, nonetheless. Ewing realized he, like the Corwinites, had a highly idealized mental image of an Earthman as a being compassionately wise, physically superb, a superman in all respects. It would be disappointing to learn that the fabled inhabitants of the legendary mother world were mere human beings themselves, like their remote descendants on the colony worlds.

Ewing strapped himself in for the downward jaunt through the atmospheric blanket of Earth and nudged the lever that controlled the autopilot. The ultimate leg of his journey had begun. Within an hour, he would actually stand on the soil of Earth herself.

I hope they'll be able to help us, he thought. Bright in his mind was a vivid mental image: faceless hordes of barbaric Klodni sweeping down on the galaxy out of Andromeda, devouring world after world in their relentless drive inward toward civilization's heart.

Already four worlds had fallen to the Klodni since the aliens had begun their campaign of conquest. The timetable said they would reach Corwin within the next decade.

Cities destroyed, women and children carried into slavery, the glittering spire of the World Building a charred ruin, the University destroyed, the fertile fields blackened by the Klodni scorched-earth tactics—

Ewing shuddered as his tiny ship spiraled Earthward, bobbing in the thickening layers of atmosphere. *Earth will help us,* he told himself comfortingly, *Earth will save her colonies from conquest.*

Ewing felt capillaries bursting under the increasing drag of deceleration. He gripped the handrests and shouted to relieve the tension on his eardrums, but there was no way of relieving the tension within. The thunder of his jets boomed through the framework of the ship, and the green planet grew frighteningly huge in the clear plastic of the view-screen. . . .

Minutes later, the ship came to rest on a broad ferroconcrete landing apron; it hung poised a moment on its own jet-wash, then settled gently to earth. With gravity-heavy fingers Ewing unfastened himself. Through the vision-screen he saw small beetle-like autotrucks come rumbling over the field toward his ship. The decontamination squad, no doubt; robot-manned of course.

He waited until they had done their job, then sprung the hatch on his ship and climbed out. The air smelled good—strange, since his home had a twenty-three percent oxygen content, two parts in a hundred richer than Earth's—and the day was warm.

Ewing spied the vaulting sweep of a terminal building, and headed toward it.

A robot, blocky and faceless, scanned him with
photo-beams as he passed through the swinging
doors. Within, the terminal was a maze of blinking
lights, red-green, on-off, up-down. Momentarily,
Ewing was dazed.

Beings of all kinds thronged the building. Ewing
saw four semi-humanoid forms with bulbous heads
engaged in a busy discussion near where he stood.
Further in the distance swarms of more Terrestrial
beings moved about. Ewing was startled by their
appearance.

Some were "normal"—oddly muscular and
rugged-looking, but not so much that they would
cause any surprised comment on Corwin. But the
others!

Dressed flamboyantly in shimmering robes of turquoise and black, gray and gold, they presented a
weird sight. One had no ears; his skull was bare,
decorated only by jeweled pendants that seemed to
be riveted to the flesh of his scalp. Another had one
leg and supported himself by a luminous crutch. A
third wore gleaming emeralds on a golden nose ring.

No two of them seemed to look alike. As a trained
student of cultural patterns, Ewing was aware of the
cause of the phenomenon; overelaboration of deco-
ration was a common evolution for highly advanced
societies, such as Earth's. But it made him feel terribly provincial to see the gaudy display. Corwin was a
new world, even after a thousand years of colonization; such fancies were yet to take root there.

Hesitantly, he approached the group of dandified

Terrestrials nearest him. They were chattering in artificial-sounding, high-pitched voices.

"Pardon," Ewing said. "I've just arrived from the Free World of Corwin. Is there some place where I can register with the authorities?"

The conversation ceased as if cut off with an ax. The trio whirled, facing Ewing. "You be from a colony world?" asked the uniped, in barely intelligible accents.

Ewing nodded. "Corwin. Sixteen parsecs away. We were settled by Earth a thousand years ago."

They exchanged words at a speed that made comprehension impossible; it seemed like a private language, some made-up doubletalk. Ewing watched the rouged faces, feeling distaste.

"Where can I register with the authorities?" he asked again, a little stiffly.

The earless one giggled shrilly. "What authorities? This is Earth, friend! We come and go as we please."

A sense of uneasiness grew in Ewing. He disliked these Terrestrials almost upon sight, after just a moment's contact.

A new voice, strange, harshly accented, said, "Did I hear you say you were from a colony?"

Ewing turned. One of the "normal" Terrestrials was speaking to him—a man about five-feet-eight, with a thick, squarish face, beetling brows looming over dark smoldering eyes, and a cropped, bullet-shaped head. His voice was dull and ugly sounding.

"I'm from Corwin," Ewing said.

The other frowned, screwing up his massive brows. He said, "Where's that?"

"Sixteen parsecs. Epsilon Ursae Majoris XII. Earth colony."

"And what are you doing on Earth?"

The belligerent tone annoyed Ewing. The Corwinite said, in a bleak voice, "I'm an officially accredited ambassador from my world to the government of Earth. I'm looking for the customs authority."

"There are none," the squat man said. "The Earthers did away with them about a century back. Couldn't be bothered with them, they said." He grinned in cheerful contempt at the three dandies, who had moved further away and were murmuring busily to each other in their private language. "The Earthers can't hardly be bothered with anything."

Ewing was puzzled. "Aren't you from Earth yourself? I mean—"

"Me?" The deep chest emitted a rumbling, sardonic chuckle. "You folk really *are* isolated, aren't you? I'm a Sirian. Sirius IV—oldest Terrestrial colony there is. Suppose we get a drink. I want to talk to you."

TWO

SOMEWHAT unwillingly, Ewing followed the burly
Sirian through the thronged terminal toward a refreshment room at the far side of the arcade. As soon
as they were seated at a gleaming translucent table,
the Sirian stared levely at Ewing and said, "First
things come first. What's your name?"

"Baird Ewing. You?"

"Rollun Firnik. What brings you to Earth,
Ewing?"

Firnik's manner was offensively blunt. Ewing
toyed with the golden-amber drink the Sirian had
bought for him, sipped it idly, put it down. "I told
you," he said quietly. "I'm an ambassador from the
government of Corwin to the government of Earth.
It's as simple as that."

"It is? When did you people last have any contact
with the rest of the galaxy?"

"Five hundred years ago. But—"

"Five hundred years," Firnik repeated specula-
tively. "And now you decide to reopen contact with

Earth.'' He squinted at Ewing, chin resting on balled fist. ''Just like that. Poof! Enter one ambassador. It isn't just out of sociability, is it, Ewing? What's the reason behind your visit?''

''I'm not familiar with the latest news in this sector of the galaxy,'' Ewing said. ''Have you heard any mention of the Klodni?''

''Klodni?'' the Sirian repeated. ''No. The name doesn't mean a thing to me. Should it?''

''News travels slowly through the galaxy,'' Ewing said. ''The Klodni are a humanoid race that evolved somewhere in the Andromeda star cluster. I've seen solidographs of them. They're little greasy creatures, about five feet high, with a sort of ant-like civilization. A war-fleet of Klodni is on the move.''

Firnik rolled an eyebrow upward. He said nothing.

''A couple thousand Klodni ships entered our galaxy about four years ago. They landed on Barnholt—that's a colony world about a hundred fifty light-years deeper in space than we are—and wiped the place clean. After about a year they picked up and moved on. They've been to four planets so far, and no one's been able to stop them yet. They swarm over a planet and destroy everything they see, then go on to the next world.''

''What of it?''

''We've plotted their probable course. They're going to attack Corwin in ten years or so, give or take one year either way. We know we can't fight them back, either. We just aren't a militarized people. And we can't militarize in less than ten years and hope to win.'' Ewing paused, sipped at his drink. It was surprisingly mild, he thought.

He went on: "As soon as the nature of the Klodni menace became known, we radioed a message to Earth explaining the situation and asking for help. We got no answer, even figuring in the subetheric lag. We radioed again. Still no reply from Earth."

"So you decided to send an ambassador," Firnik said. "Figuring your messages must have gone astray, no doubt. You wanted to negotiate for help at first hand."

"Yes."

The Sirian chuckled. "You know something? It's three hundred years since anybody on Earth last fired anything deadlier than a popgun. They're total pacifists."

"That can't be true!"

Suddenly the sardonic amiability left Firnik. His voice was almost toneless as he said, "I'll forgive you this time, because you're a stranger and don't know the customs. But the next time you call me a liar I'll kill you."

Ewing's jaw stiffened. *Barbarian,* he thought. Out loud he said, "In other words, I've wasted my time by coming here, then?"

The Sirian shrugged unconcernedly. "Better fight your own battles. The Earthers can't help you."

"But they're in danger too," Ewing protested. "Do you think the Klodni are going to stop before they've reached Earth?"

"How long do you think it'll take them to get as far as Earth?" Firnik asked.

"A century at least."

"A century. All right. They have to pass through Sirius IV on their way to Earth. We'll take care of them when the time comes.''

And I came sixteen parsecs across the galaxy to ask for help, Ewing thought.

He stood up. ''It's been very interesting talking to you. And thanks for the drink.''

''Good luck to you,'' the Sirian said in parting. It was not meant in a spirit of cheer. It sounded openly derisive, Ewing thought.

He made his way through the crowded room to the long shining-walled corridor of the spaceport arcade. A ship was blasting off outside on the ferroconcrete apron; Ewing watched it a moment as it thundered out of sight. He realized that if any truth lay in the Sirian's words, he might just as well return to Corwin now and report failure.

But it was hard to accept the concept of a decadent, spineless Earth. True, they had had no contact with the mother world for five centuries; but the legend still gleamed on Corwin and the other colony worlds of its immediate galactic area—the legend of the mother planet where human life first began, hundreds of centuries before.

He remembered the stories of the pioneers of space, the first bold venturers to the other planets, then the brave colonists who had extended Earth's sway to half a thousand worlds. Through a natural process, contact with the homeland had withered in the span of years; there was little reason for self-sufficient worlds a sky apart to maintain anything as fantastically expensive as interstellar communication systems simply for reasons of sentiment. A colony world has economic problems as it is.

There had always been the legend of Earth,

though, to guide the Corwinites. When trouble arose, Earth would be there to help.

Now there was trouble on the horizon. And Earth, Ewing thought? Can we count on her help?

He watched the throngs of bejeweled dandies glumly, and wondered.

He paused by a railing that looked out over the wide sweep of the spacefield. A plaque, copper-hued, proclaimed the fact that this particular section of the arcade had been erected A.D. 2716. Ewing, a newcomer in an ancient world, felt a tingle of awe. The building in which he stood had been constructed more than a century before the first ships from Earth blasted down on Corwin, which then had been only a nameless world on the star charts. And the men who had built this building, eleven hundred years ago, were as remote in space-time from the present-day Terrans as were the people of Corwin at this moment.

It was a bitter thought, that he had wasted his trip. There was his wife, and his son—for more than two years Laira would have no husband, Blade no father. And for what? All for a wasted trip to a planet whose glories lay far in its past?

Somewhere on Earth, he thought, *there will be someone who can help. This planet produced us all. A shred of vitality must remain in it somewhere. I won't leave without trying to find it.*

Some painstaking questioning of one of the stationary robot guards finally got him the information he wanted: there *was* a place where incoming outworlders could register if they chose. He made provisions for the care and storage of his ship until his departure, and signed himself in at the Hall of Records as Baird Ewing, Ambassador from the Free World of Corwin. There was a hotel affiliated with the spaceport terminal; Ewing requested and was assigned a room in it. He signed a slip granting the robot spaceport attendants permission to enter his ship and transfer his personal belongings to his hotel room.

The room was attractive, if a little cramped. Ewing was accustomed to the spaciousness of his home on Corwin, a planet on which only eighteen million people lived in an area greater than the habitable landmass of Earth. He had helped to build the home himself, twelve years ago when he married Laira. It sprawled over nearly eleven acres of land. To be confined to a room only about fifteen feet on a side was a novel experience for him.

The lighting was subdued and indirect; he searched for the source unsuccessfully. His fingers probed the walls, but no electroluminescent panels were in evidence. The Earthers had evidently developed some new technique for diffused multi-source lighting.

An outlet covered with a speaking grid served as his connection with the office downstairs. He switched the communicator panel on, after some inward deliberation. A robot voice said immediately, "How may we serve you, Mr. Ewing?"

"Is there such a thing as a library on the premises?"

"Yes, sir."

"Good. Would you have someone select a volume of Terran history covering the last thousand years, and have it sent up to me. Also any recent newspapers, magazines, or things like that.''

''Of course, sir.''

It seemed that hardly five minutes passed before the chime on his room door bleeped discreetly.

''Come in,'' he said.

The door had been attuned to the sound of his voice; as he spoke, there was the whispering sound of relays closing, and the door whistled open. A robot stood just outside. His flat metal arms were stacked high with microreels.

''You ordered reading matter, sir.''

''Thanks. Would you leave them over there, near the viewer?''

When the robot had gone, he lifted the most massive reel from the stack and scanned its title. *Earth and the Galaxy* was the title. In smaller letters it said, *A Study in Colonial Relationships*.

Ewing nodded approvingly. This was the way to begin, he told himself: fill in the background before embarking on any specific course of action. The mocking Sirian had perhaps underestimated Earth's strength deliberately, for obscure reasons of his own. He did not seem like a trustworthy sort.

He opened the reel and slid it into the viewer, twisting it until he heard the familiar *click!* The viewer was of the same model in use on Corwin, and he had no difficulties with it. He switched on the screen; the title page appeared, and a moment's work with the focusing switches rendered the image brightly sharp.

Chapter One, he read. *The earliest period of expansion.*

The Age of Interstellar Colonization may rightly

be said to have opened in the year 2560, when the development of the Haley Subwarp Drive made possible —

The door chimed again. Irritated, Ewing looked up from his book. He was not expecting visitors, nor had he asked the hotel service staff for anything.

"Who is it?"

"Mr. Ewing?" said a familiar voice. "Might I come in? I'd like to talk to you again. We met briefly at the terminal this afternoon."

Ewing recognized the voice. It belonged to the earless Earther in turquoise robes who had been so little help to him earlier. *What can he want with me?* Ewing wondered.

"All right," he said. "Come in."

The door responded to the command. It slid back obediently. The slim Terrestrial smiled apologetically at Ewing, murmured a soft greeting, and entered.

THREE

HE WAS slim, delicate, fragile-looking. It seemed to Ewing that a good gust of wind would smash him to splinters. He was no more than five feet tall, pale, waxy skinned, with large serious eyes and thin, indecisive lips. His domed skull was naked and faintly glossly. At regular intervals on its skin, jeweled pendants had been surgically attached; they jiggled as he moved.

With prim fastidiousness he made his way across the room toward Ewing.

"I hope I'm not intruding on your privacy," he said in a hesitant half-whisper.

"No. Not at all. Won't you be seated?"

"I would prefer to stand," the Earther replied. "It is our custom."

"Very well."

Ewing felt a curious inner revulsion as he stared at the grotesque little Earther. On Corwin, anyone dressed in such clownish garb would meet with derision.

The Earther smiled timidly. "I am called Scholar

Myreck,'' he said finally. ''And you are Baird Ewing, of the colony-world Corwin.''

''That's right.''

''It was my great fortune to meet you at the spaceport terminal building earlier today. Apparently I created a bad first impression—one of frivolity, perhaps, or even of oppressive irresponsibility. For this I wish to beg your pardon, Colonist Ewing. I would have had the opportunity then, but for that Sirian ape who seized your attention before I could speak.''

Somewhat to his surprise Ewing noticed that the little Earther was speaking with barely a trace of what he had come to regard as the Earther accent. He frowned; what did the foppish little man want?

''On the contrary, Scholar Myreck, no apologies should be needed. I don't judge a man by my first impression of him—especially on a world where I'm a stranger to the customs and way of life.''

''An excellent philosophy!'' Sadness crossed Myreck's mild face for a moment. ''But you look tense, Colonist Ewing. Might I have the privilege of relaxing you?''

''Relaxing me?''

''Minor neural adjustments; a technique we practice with some skill here. May I?''

Doubtfully Ewing said, ''Just what does it involve, actually?''

''A moment's physical contact, nothing more.'' Myreck smiled imploringly. ''It pains me to see a man so tense. It causes me actual physical pain.''

''You've aroused my curiosity,'' Ewing said. ''Go ahead—relax me.''

Myreck glided forward and put his hands gently round Ewing's neck. The Corwinite stiffened in immediate alarm. "Gently," Myreck sang. "Let the muscles relax. Don't fight me. Relax."

His thin, childlike fingers dug in without warning, pinching sharply at the base of Ewing's skull. Ewing felt a quick, fierce burst of light, a jarring disruption of sense-perception, for no more than a fifteenth of a second. Then, suddenly, he felt the tension drain away from him. His deltoids and trapezoids eased so abruptly that he thought his back and shoulders had been removed. His neck, chronically stiff, loosened. The stress patterns developed during a year in stasis-sleep were shaken off.

"That's quite a trick," he said finally.

"We manipulate the neural nexus at the point where the medulla and the spinal column become one. In the hands of an amateur it can be fatal." Myreck smiled. "In the hands of a professional such as myself it can also be fatal—but only when the operator so intends."

Ewing moistened his lips. He said, "May I ask a personal question, Scholar Myreck?"

"Of course."

"The clothes you wear—the ornamentation—are these things widespread on Earth, or is it just some fad that you're following?"

Myreck knotted his waxy fingers together thoughtfully. "They are, shall we say, cultural manifestations. I find it hard to explain. People of my personality type and inclinations dress this way; others dress differently, as the mood strikes them. My appearance indicates that I am a Collegiate Fellow."

"Scholar is your title, then?"

"Yes. And also my given name. I am a member of the College of Abstract Science of the City of Valloin."

"I'll have to plead ignorance," Ewing said. "I don't know anything about your College."

"Understandable. We do not seek publicity." Myreck's eyes fastened doggedly on Ewing's for a moment. "That Sirian who took you away from us—may I ask his name?"

"Rollun Firnik," Ewing said.

"A particularly dangerous one; I know him by reputation. Well, to the point at last, Colonist Ewing. Would you care to address a convocation of the College of Abstract Science some time early next week?"

"I? I'm no academician, Scholar. I wouldn't know what to talk about."

"You come from a colony, one that none of us knows anything about. You offer an invaluable fund of experience and information."

"But I'm a stranger in the city," Ewing objected. "I wouldn't know how to get to you."

"We will arrange for your transportation. The meeting is Fournight of next week. Will you come?"

Ewing considered it for a moment. It was as good an opportunity as any to begin studying the Terrestrial culture at close range. He would need as broad and as deep a fund of knowledge as possible in order to apply the leverage that would ultimately preserve his home world from destruction by the alien marauders.

He looked up. "All right. Fournight of next week it is, then."

"We will be very grateful, Colonist Ewing."

Myreck bowed. He backed toward the door, smiling and nodding, and paused just before pushing the opener stud. "Stay well," he said. "You have our extreme gratitude. We will see you on Fournight."

The door slid closed behind him.

Ewing shrugged; then, remembering the reels he had requested from the hotel library, he returned his attention to the viewer.

He read for nearly an hour, skimming; his reading pace was an accelerated one, thanks to his mnemonic training at the great University of Corwin. His mind efficiently organized the material as fast as his eyes scanned it, marshaling the facts into near, well-drilled columns. By the end of the hour, he had more than a fair idea of the shape of Terrestrial history in the thirteen hundred years since the first successful interstellar flight.

There had been an immediate explosive outward push to the stars. Sirius had been the first to be colonized, in 2573: sixty-two brave men and women. The other colonies had followed fast, frantically. The overcrowded Earth was shipping her sons and daughters to the stars in wholesale batches.

All through the second half of the Third Millennium the prevailing historical tone was one of frenzied excitement. The annals listed colony after colony.

The sky was full of worlds. The seventeen planet system of Aldebaran yielded eight Earth-type planets suitable for Colonization. The double system of Albireo had four. Ewing passed hastily over the name-weighted pages, seeing with a little quiver of recognition the name of Blade Corwin, who seeded a colony on Epsilon Ursae Majoris XII in the year 2856.

Outward. *By the opening of the thirtieth century,* said the book, *human life had been planted on more than a thousand worlds of the universe.*

The great outward push was over. On Earth, the long-over-due establishment of population controls had ended forever the threat of overexpansion, with it some of the impetus for colonization died. Earth's population stabilized itself at an unvarying five and a half billion; three centuries before, nearly eleven billion had jostled for room on the crowded little planet.

With population stabilization came cultural stabilization, the end of the flamboyant pioneer personality, the development of a new kind of Earthman who lacked the drive and intense ambition of his ancestors. The colonies had skimmed off the men with outward drive; the ones who remained on Earth gave rise to a culture of esthetes, of debaters and musicians and mathematicians. A subclass of menials at first sprang up to insure the continued maintenance of the machinery of civilization, but even these became unnecessary with the development of ambulatory robots.

The history of the Fourth Millennium was a predictable one; Ewing had already extrapolated it from the data given him, and it was little surprise to come across confirmation. There had been retrenchment. The robot-served culture of Earth became self-sufficient, a closed system. Births and deaths were carefully equalized.

With stability came isolation. The wild men on the

colony worlds no longer had need for the mother world, nor Earth for them. Contacts withered.

In the year 3800, said the text, *only Sirius IV of all Earth's colonies still retained regular communication with the parent planet. Representatives of the thousand other colonies were so rare on Earth as to be virtually nonexistent there.*

Only Sirius IV. It was odd, thought Ewing, that of all the colonies the harsh people of Sirius IV should alone be solicitous of the mother world. There was little in common between Rollun Firnik and the Scholar.

The more Ewing read, the less confident he became that he would find any aid for Corwin here. Earth had become a planet of gentle scholiasts, it seemed; was there anything here that could serve in the struggle against the advancing Klodni?

Possibly not. But Ewing did not intend to abandon his quest at its very beginning.

He read on, well into the afternoon, until he felt hunger. Rising, he disconnected the viewer and rewound the reels, slipping them back into their containers. His eyes were tired. Some of the physical fatigue Myreck had taken from him had begun to steal back into his body.

There was a restaurant on the sixty-third level of the hotel, according to the printed information sheet enameled on the inside of his door. He showered and dressed formally, in his second-best doublet and lace. He checked the chambers of his ceremonial blaster, found them all functioning, and strapped the weapon to his hip. Satisfied at last, he reached for the housephone, and when the subservient roboperator answered said, "I'm going to eat dinner now. Will you notify the hotel dining room to reserve a table for one for me?"

"Of course, Mr. Ewing."

He broke the contact and glanced once again in the mirror above his dresser to make sure his face was in order. He felt in his pocket for his wallet; bulged with Terrestrial paper money, enough to last him the length of his stay.

He opened the door. Just outside the door was an opaque plastic receptacle which was used for depositing messages and to Ewing's surprise the red light atop it was glowing, indicating the presence of a message within.

Pressing his thumb to the identiplate, he lifted the top of the box and drew out the note. It was neatly typed in blue capital letters. It said:

COLONIST EWING: IF YOU WANT TO STAY IN GOOD HEALTH, KEEP AWAY FROM MYRECK AND HIS FRIENDS.

It was unsigned. Ewing smiled coldly; the intrigue was beginning already, the jockeying back and forth. He had expected it. The arrival of a strange colonial on Earth was a novel enough event; it was sure to have its consequences and repercussions as his presence became more widely known.

"Open," he said shortly to his door.

The door slid back. He reentered his room and snatched up the house phone.

The desk robot said, "How may we serve you, Mr. Ewing?"

"There seems to be a spy vent in my room some

place," Ewing said. "Send someone up to check the room over, will you?"

"I assure you, sir that no such thing could—"

"I tell you there's a concealed camera or microphone someplace in my room. Either find it or I'll check into some other hotel."

"Yes, Mr. Ewing. We'll send an investigator up immediately."

"Good. I'm going to the dining room, now. If anything turns up, contact me there."

FOUR

THE HOTEL dining room was gaudily, even garishly decorated. Glowing spheres of imprisoned radiant energy drifted at random near the vaulted ceiling, occasionally bobbing down to eye level. The tables themselves were banked steeply toward the outside edge, and in the very center of the room, where the floor level was lowest, a panchromaticon swiveled slowly, casting multicolored light over the diners.

A burnished, bullet-headed robot waited at the door.

"I have a reservation," Ewing said. "Baird Ewing. Room 4113."

"Of course, sir. Come this way, please."

Ewing followed the robot into the main concourse of the dining room, up a sort of ramp that led to the outermost rim of the great hall, where a few empty tables were visible. The robot came to a halt in front of a table at which someone was already sitting: a Sirian girl, Ewing guessed, from her brawny appearance.

The robot pulled out the chair facing her. Ewing shook his head. "There's been some mistake made. I don't know this lady at all. I requested a table for one.''

"We ask indulgence, sir. There are no tables for one available at this hour. We consulted with the person occupying this table and were told that there was no objection to your sharing it, if you were willing to do so.''

Ewing frowned and glanced at the girl. She met his glance evenly, and smiled. She seemed to be inviting him to sit down.

He shrugged. "All right. I'll sit here.''

"Very good, sir.''

Ewing slipped into the seat and let the robot nudge it toward the table for him. He looked at the girl. She had bright red hair, trimmed in what on Corwin would be considered an extremely mannish style. She was dressed in a tailored suit of some clinging purple material; it flared sharply at the shoulders and neck. Her eyes were dark black. Her face was broad and muscular looking, with upjutting cheekbones that gave her features an oddly slant-eyed cast.

"I'm sorry if I caused you any inconvenience,'' Ewing said. "I had no idea they'd place me at your table—or at any occupied table.''

"I requested it,'' she said. Her voice was dark of timbre and resonant. "You're the Corwinite Ewing, I understand. I'm Byra Clork. We have something in common. We were both born on colonies of Earth.''

Ewing found himself liking her blunt, forthright approach, even though in her countryman Firnik it had been offensive. He said, "So I understand. You're a Sirian, aren't you?''

"That's right. How did you know?''

28

"I guessed," Ewing said evasively. He directed his attention to the liquor panel set against the wall. "Drink?" he asked her.

"I've had one. But I don't mind if you do."

Ewing inserted a coin and punched out a cocktail. The drink emerged from a revolving slot in the wall. The Corwinite picked it up and tasted it. It was sweet, with a disturbing undertaste of acridity.

"You said you requested my presence at your table," Ewing remarked. "And you knew me by name. How come?"

"It isn't every day that a stranger comes to Earth," she said, in that impossibly deep, husky, almost-masculine voice. "I was curious."

"Many people seem to be curious about me," Ewing said.

A robowaiter hovered at his shoulder. Ewing frowned; he said, "I don't have any idea what the speciality of the house is. Miss Clork, would you care to recommend something for my dinner?"

She said to the robot, "Give him the same thing I ordered. Venison, creamed potatoes, green beans."

"Certainly," murmured the robot. As it scuttled away Ewing said, "Is that the tastiest dish they have?"

"Probably. I know it's the most expensive."

Ewing grinned. "You don't spare my pocketbook, do you?"

"You gave me free reign. Besides, you must have some money in your pocket. I saw you converting a stack of bills at the desk this morning."

"You saw me, then?" An idea struck him. "You didn't send me a note this afternoon, did you?"

"Note?" Her broad face showed seemingly, genuine confusion. "No, I didn't send you any note. Why?"

"Someone did," Ewing said. "I just wondered who it might have been."

He sipped his drink thoughtfully. A few minutes later a robot arrived with their dinners. The meat smelled pungent and good. Obviously it was no synthetic; that explained its high cost.

They ate in silence for a while. When Ewing had made substantial inroads on his plate, he paused, looking up, and said, "What do you do on Earth, Miss Clork?"

She smiled. "I'm with the Sirian Consulate. I look out for the interests of any of my people who happen to visit Earth. It's a very dull job."

"There seem to be quite a few Sirians on Earth," Ewing remarked casually. "It must be very popular among your people as a tourist attraction."

She seemed momentarily disconcerted by Ewing's remark. Her voice hesitated slightly as she said, "Y-yes, it's very popular. Many Sirians like to vacation on Earth."

"How many Sirians would you say there were on Earth right now?"

This time she stiffened visibly; Ewing realized he had accidently asked a question which touched on very delicate grounds. "Just why are you interested, Colonist Ewing?"

He smiled disarmingly. "A matter of curiosity, that's all. No ulterior motives."

She pretended the question had never been asked. Music welled up about them, blending with the vague general hum of conversation. She finished her dinner quietly, and while starting on the dessert said, "I suppose you didn't think much of Firnik."

"Of who?"

"You met him this morning," she said. "The Sirian. He tends to be rather clumsy at times. He's my boss, actually. Sirian Vice-Consul in Valloin."

"Did he tell you to wangle dinner with me?" Ewing asked suddenly.

A blaze flamed in the Sirian girl's eyes, but it died down quickly enough, though with reluctance. "You put things crudely."

"But accurately?"

"Yes."

Ewing smiled and reached into his doublet pocket; he drew forth the annonymous note he had received earlier, unfolded it, and shoved it across the table toward her. She read it without displaying any apparent reaction, and nudged it back toward him.

"Is this the note you suspected me of having sent you?" she asked.

Ewing nodded. "I had a visit from Scholar Myreck this afternoon. Several hours later I found this note outside my door. Perhaps Vice-Consul Firnik sent it, eh?"

She stared at him as if trying to read his mind. Ewing sensed that a chess game of sorts was going on, that he was rapidly becoming the center of a web of complications. While they stared silently at each other a robot glided up to them and said, "Mr. Ewing?"

"That's right."

"I bear a message from the manager of the hotel."

"Let's have it," Ewing said.

"The message is: a spyvent outlet has been discovered in your room at the intersection of the wall and the ceiling. The outlet has been removed and a protective device planted in the room to prevent any future re-insertion of spying equipment. The manager extends his deep regrets and requests you to accept a week's rent as partial compensation for any inconvenience this may have caused you."

Ewing grinned. "Tell him I accept the offer, and that he'd better be more careful about his rooms the next time."

When the robot was gone, Ewing stared sharply at Byra Clork and said, "Somebody was listening and watching today when I had my visitor. Was it Firnik?"

"Do you think so?"

"I do."

"Then so be it," the girl said lightly. She rose from the table and said, "Do you mind putting my meal on your account? I'm a little short of cash just now."

She started to leave. Ewing caught a robot's eye and quickly instructed, "Bill me for both dinners. Ewing, room 4113."

He slid past the metal creature and caught up with the Sirian girl as she approached the exit to the dining room. The sphincter-door widened; she stepped through, and he followed her. They emerged in a luxurious salon hung with abstract paintings of startling texture and hue. Fierce atonal music came pulsing out of speakers concealed near the paintings.

She was ignoring him, pointedly. She moved at a rapid pace down the main corridor of the salon, and stopped just before an inlaid blue-and-gold door. As she started to enter, Ewing grasped her by the arm. Her biceps were remarkably sturdy.

She wriggled loose and said, "Surely you don't intend to follow me in *here*, Mr. Ewing!"

He glanced at the inscription on the door. "I'm a rude, untutored, primitive colonial," he said grimly. "If it serves my purpose to go in there after you, I'll go in there after you. You might just as well stay here and answer my questions as try to run away."

"Is there any reason why I should?"

"Yes," he said. "Because I ask you to. Did you or Firnik spy on me this afternoon?"

"How should I know what Firnik does in his free time?"

Ewing applied pressure to her arm, and at the same time silently recited verses designed to keep his own inward metabolism on a level keel during a time of stress. His pulse was pounding; methodically, he forced it to return to its normal rate.

"You're hurting me," she said in a harsh whisper.

"I want to know who planted that spy ray in my room, and why I should be warned against dealing with Myreck."

She twisted suddenly and broke loose from his grasp. Her face was flushed, and her breathing was rapid and irregular. In a low voice she said, "Let me give you some free advice, Mr. Corwinite Ewing. Pack up and go back to Corwin. There's only trouble for you on Earth."

"What sort of trouble?" he demanded relentlessly.

"I'm not saying anything else. Listen to me, and

get as far from Earth as you can. Tomorrow. Today, if you can.'' She looked wildly around, then turned and ran lithely down the corridor. Ewing debated following her, but decided against it. She had seemed genuinely frightened, as if trouble loomed for her.

He stood for a moment before a mounted light-sculpture, pretending to be staring at the intertwining spirals of black and pearl-gray, but actually merely using the statuary as pretext for a moment's thought. His mind was racing; rigidly, he forced his adrenalin count down. When he was calm again, he tried to evaluate the situation.

Someone had gimmicked his room. He had been visited by an Earther, and a Sirian girl had maneuvered him into eating dinner with her. The incidents were beginning to mount up, and they grew more puzzling as he attempted to fit them into some coherent pattern. He had been on Earth less than fifteen hours. Events moved rapidly here.

He had been trained in theories of synthesis; he was a gifted extrapolator. Sweat beaded his forehead as he labored to extract connectivity from the isolated and confusing incidents of the day.

Minutes passed. Earthers in dazzling costumes drifted past him in twos and sometimes threes, commenting in subued tones on the displays in the salon. Painstakingly, Ewing manipulated the facts. Finally a picture took shape; a picture formed on guesswork, but nonetheless a useful guide to future action.

The Sirians were up to no good on Earth. Quite possibly they intended to make the mother world a Sirian dominion. Assuming that, then the unexpected arrival of a colonist from deep space might represent a potential threat to their plans.

New shadows darkened the horizon, Ewing saw. Perhaps Firnik suspected him of intending to conspire with the Scholars against the Sirians. Doubtless that had been Myreck's intention in proffering the invitation.

In that case—

"Mr. Ewing?" a gentle voice said.

He turned. A robot stood there, man-high, armless, its face a sleek sheet of viewing plastic.

"That's right, I'm Ewing. What is it?"

"I speak for Governor-General Mellis, director of Earth's governing body. Governor-General Mellis requests your presence at the Capital City as soon as is convenient for you."

"How do I get there?"

"If you wish I will convey you there," the robot purred.

"I so wish," Ewing said. "Take me there at once."

FIVE

A JETCAR waited outside the hotel for them—sleek, stylishly toned, and yet to Ewing's eyes old-fashioned in appearance. The robot opened the rear door and Ewing climbed in.

To his surprise the robot did not join him inside the car; he simply closed the door and glided away into the gathering dusk. Ewing frowned and peered through the door window at the retreating robot. He rattled the doorknob experimentally and discovered that he was locked in.

A bland robot voice said, "Your destination, please?"

Ewing hesitated. "Ah—take me to Governor-General Mellis."

A rumble of turbogenerators was the only response; the car quivered gently and slid forward, moving as if it ran on a track of oil. Ewing felt no perceptible sensation of motion, but the spaceport and the towering bulk of the hotel grew small behind him, and soon they emerged on a broad twelve-level superhighway a hundred feet above the ground level.

Ewing stared nervously out the window. "Exactly where *is* the Governor-General located?" he asked, turning to peer at the dashboard. The jetcar did not even have room for a driver, he noted, nor a set of manual controls. It was operated totally by remote control.

"Governor-General Mellis' residence is in Capital City," came the precise, measured reply. "It is located one hundred ninety-three miles to the north of the City of Valloin. We will be there in forty-one minutes."

The jetcar was strict in its schedule. Exactly forty-one minutes after it had pulled away from the plaza facing the Grand Valloin Hotel, it shot off the highway and onto a smaller trunk road that plunged downward at a steep angle. Ewing saw a city before him—a city of spacious buildings spaced far apart, radiating spirally out from one towering, silver-hued palace.

A few minutes later the car came to a sudden halt, giving Ewing a mild jolt.

The robot voice said, "This is the palace of the Governor-General. The door at your left is open. Please leave the car now and you will be taken to the Governor-General."

Ewing nudged the door-panel and it swung open. He stepped out. The night air was fresh and cool, and the street about him gave off a soft gentle glow. Accumulator batteries beneath the pavement were discharging the illumination the sun had shed on them during the day.

"You will come this way, please," a new robot said.

He was ushered speedily and efficiently through

the swinging door of the palace, into a lift, and upward. The lift opened out onto a velvet-hung corridor that extended through a series of accordion-like pleats into a large and austerely furnished room.

A small man stood alone in the center of the room. He was gray haired but unwrinkled, and his body bore no visual sign of the surgical distortions that were so common among the Earthers. He smiled courteously.

"I am Governor-General Mellis," he said. His voice was light and flexible, a good vehicle for public speaking. "Will you come in?"

"Thanks," Ewing said. He stepped inside. The doors immediately closed behind him.

Mellis came forward—he stood no higher than the middle of Ewing's chest—and proffered a drink. Ewing took it. It was a sparkling purplish liquid, with a mildly carbonated texture. He settled himself comfortably in the chair Mellis drew up for him, and looked up at the Governor-General, who remained standing.

"You wasted no time in sending for me," Ewing remarked.

The Governor-General shrugged gracefully. "I learned of your arrival this morning. It is not often that an ambassador from an outworld colony arrives on Earth. In truth"—he seemed to sigh—"you are the first in more than three hundred years. You have aroused considerable curiosity, you know."

"I'm aware of that." Casually he sipped at his drink, letting the warmth trickle down his throat. "I intended to contact you tomorrow, or perhaps the next day. But you've saved me that trouble."

"My curiosity got the better of me," Mellis admitted with a smile. "There is so little for me to do, you see, in the way of official duties."

"I'll make my visit brief by starting at the beginning," Ewing said. "I'm here to ask for Earth's help, in behalf of my planet, the Free World of Corwin."

"Help?" The Governor-General looked alarmed.

"We face invasion by extra-galactic foes," Ewing said. Quickly he sketched out an account of the Klodni depredations thus far, adding, "And we sent several messages to Earth to let you know what the situation was. We assume those messages have gone astray en route. And so I've come in person to ask for Earth's aid."

Mellis moved about the room in impatient birdlike strutting motions before replying. He whirled suddenly, then calmed himself, and said, "The messages did not go astray, Mr. Ewing."

"No?"

"They were duly received and forwarded to my office. I read them!"

"You didn't answer," Ewing interrupted accusingly. "You deliberately ignored them. Why?"

Mellis spread his fingers on his thighs and seemed to come stiffly to attention. In a quiet, carefully modulated voice he said, "Because there is no possible way we can help you or anyone else, Mr. Ewing. Will you believe that?"

"I don't understand."

"We have no weapons, no military forces, no ability or desire to fight. We have no spaceships."

Ewing's eyes widened. He had found it impossible to believe it when the Sirian Firnik had told him

Earth was defenseless; but to hear it from the lips of the Governor-General himself!

"There must be some assistance Earth can give. There are only eighteen million of us on Corwin," Ewing said. "We have a defense corps, of course, but it's hardly adequate. Our stockpile of nuclear weapons is low—"

"Ours is nonexistent," Mellis interrupted. "Such fissionable material as we have is allocated to operation of the municipal atom piles."

Ewing stared at the tips of his fingers. Chill crept over him, reminding him of the year spent locked in the grip of frost as he slept through a crossing of fifty light-years. For nothing.

Mellis smiled sadly. "There is one additional aspect to your request for help. You say the Klodni will not attack your world for a decade, nor ours for a century."

Ewing nodded.

"In that case," Mellis said, "the situation becomes academic from our viewpoint. Before a decade's time has gone by, Earth will be a Sirian protectorate anyway. We will be in no position to help anybody."

The Corwinite looked up at the melancholy face of Earth's Governor-General. There were depths to Mellis' eyes that told Ewing much; Mellis was deeply conscious of his position as ruler in the declining days of Terrestrial power.

Ewing said, "How sure can you be of that?"

"Certain as I am of my name," Mellis replied. "The Sirians are infiltrating Earth steadily. There are more than a million of them here now. Any day I expect to be notified that I am no longer even to be Earth's figurehead.''

"Can't you prevent them from coming to Earth?''

Mellis shook his head. "We're powerless. The events to come are inevitable. And so your Klodni worry us very little, friend Corwinite. I'll be long since dead before they arrive—and with me Earth's glories.''

"And you don't care about the colony worlds?'' Ewing snapped angrily. "You'll just sit back and let us be gobbled up by the aliens? Earth's name still means something among the colony worlds; if you issued a general declaration of war, all the colonies would send forces to defend us. As it is, the scattered worlds can't think of the common good; they only worry about themselves. They don't see that if they band together against the Klodni they can destroy them, while singly they will be overwhelmed. A declaration from Earth—''

"—would be meaningless, hollow, invalid, null, void, and empty,'' Mellis said. "Believe that, Mr. Ewing. You face an unfortunate fate. Officially, I weep for you. But as an old man soon to be pushed from his throne, I can't help you.''

Ewing felt the muscles of his jaw tighten. He said nothing. He realized there was nothing at all for him to say.

He stood up. "I guess we've reached the end of our interview, then. I'm sorry to have taken up your time, Governor-General Mellis. If I had known the situation as it stood on Earth, perhaps I might not have made this trip across space.''

"I had hoped—'' Mellis began. He broke off, then

shook his head. "No. It was foolish."

"Sir?"

The older man smiled palely. "There had been a silly thought in my mind today, ever since I learned that an ambassador from Corwin had landed in Valloin. I see clearly now how wild a thought it was."

"Might I ask—"

Mellis shrugged. "The thought I had was that perhaps you had come in the name of Terrestrial independence—to offer us a pledge of your world's aid against the encroachments of the Sirians. But you need aid yourself. It was foolish of me to expect to find a defender in the stars."

"I'm sorry," Ewing said quietly.

"For what? For being unable to help? We owe each other apologies, in that case." Mellis shook his head. "We have known brightness too long. Now the shadows start to lengthen. Aliens steal forth out of Andromeda to destroy, and children of Earth turn on their mother."

He peered through the increasing gloom of the room at Ewing. "But I must be boring you with my ramblings Mr. Ewing. You had better leave, now. Leave Earth, I mean. Go to defend your homeworld against its enemies. We are beyond help."

He pulled a wall switch and a robot servitor appeared, gliding noiselessly through the opening doors. The Governor-General turned to it.

"Conduct Mr. Ewing back to the car, and see that he is transported to his residence in Valloin as comfortably as possible."

Ewing felt a flood of pity for the old man whose misfortune it was to hold the supreme office of Earth at this dark time. He clenched his fists; he said nothing. Corwin now seemed strangely remote. His wife, his son, living under the menace of alien hordes, hardly mattered now compared with Earth and the fate, less violent but more painful, that was befalling it.

In silence he left the old man and followed the robot through the corridors to the lift. He descended on a shaft of magnetic radiance to the street level.

The car was waiting for him. He got in; the turbos thrummed briefly and the homeward journey began.

He amused himself on the way home by drafting the text of the message he would send via subradio to Corwin in the morning. In the afternoon he would leave Earth forever, setting out on the year-long return trip to Corwin, bring with him sad confirmation of the fact that there was no help for them against the Klodni horde.

SIX

IT WAS past midnight when Ewing stepped out of the lift-shaft on the forty-first floor of the Grand Valloin Hotel. He reached his room and examined the message box. Empty. He had half expected to find another threatening note in it.

He pressed his thumb to the identity-attuned plate of the door and said in a low voice, pitched so it would not awaken any of his neighbors, "Open."

The door rolled back. Unexpectedly, the light was on in his room.

"Hello," said Byra Clork.

Ewing froze in the doorway and stared bewilderedly at the broad-shouldered Sirian girl. She was sitting quite calmly in the relaxochair by the window. A bottle of some kind rested on the night table, and next to it two glasses, one of them half filled with amber liquid. She had made herself quite comfortable, it seemed.

He stepped inside.

"How did you get into my room?" he asked.

"I asked the management to give me a pass key to your room. They obliged."

"Just like that?" Ewing snapped. "I guess I don't understand the way Terrestrial hotels operated. I was under the innocent impression that a man's room was his own so long as he paid the rent, and that no strangers would be permitted to enter."

"That's the usual custom," she said lightly. "But I found it necessary to talk to you about urgent matters. Matters of great importance to the Sirian Consulate in Valloin, whom I represent."

Ewing became aware of the fact that he was holding the door open. He released it, and it closed automatically. "It's a little late in the evening for conducting Consulate business, isn't it?" he asked.

She smiled. "It's never too late for some things. Would you like a drink?"

He ignored the glass she held out to him. He wanted her to leave his room.

"How did you get in my room?" he repeated.

She pointed behind him, to the enameled sheet of regulations behind the door. "It's up there plainly enough on your door. I'll quote, in case you haven't read the regulations yet: *'The management of this Hotel reserves the right to enter and inspect any of the rooms at any time.'* I'm carrying out an inspection."

"You're not the management!"

"I'm employed by the management," she said sweetly. She dug into the reticule suspended from her left wrist and produced a glossy yellow card which she handed over to the puzzled Ewing.

He read it.

ROLLUN FIRNIK
Manager, Grand Valloin Hotel

"What does this mean?"

"It means that the robots at the desk are directly responsible to Firnik. He runs this hotel. Sirian investors bought it eight years ago, and delegated him to act as their on-the-spot representative. And in turn he delegated me to visit you in your room tonight. Now that everything's nice and legal, Ewing, sit down and let's talk. Relax."

Uncertainly Ewing slipped off his coat and sat down on the edge of the bed, facing her.

"We've had one conversation already today, haven't we? A highly inconclusive and fragmentary one, which ended when—"

"Forget about that!"

The sudden whiteness of her face told him one thing he had been anxious to know: they were being watched. He had nearly revealed something she had not wanted the watchers to find out.

"I—have different instructions now," she said hesitantly. "Won't you have a drink?"

He shook his head. "I've already had more than my share today, thanks. And I'm tired. Now that you've gotten in here, suppose you tell me what you want."

"You visited Governor-General Mellis tonight, didn't you?" she asked abruptly.

"Did I?"

"You don't have to be mysterious about it," she said sharply. "You were seen leaving and returning in an official car. Don't waste your breath by denying you had an interview with the Governor-General."

Ewing shrugged. "How would it concern you, assuming that I did?"

"To be perfectly frank with you, Mr. Ewing, your

46

presence on Earth worries us. By *us* I mean the interests of the Sirian government, whom I represent. We have a definite financial interest in Earth. We don't want to see that investment jeopardized.''

Ewing frowned in curiosity. ''You haven't made things much clearer,'' he said.

''Briefly, we wondered whether or not you—representing Corwin or possibly a league of the outworld colonies—have territorial designs on Earth,'' she said slowly. ''I've been utterly blunt, now. Too blunt, perhaps. We Sirians are poor at diplomacy; we have a racial characteristic of always coming directly to the point.''

''Corwinites share that characteristic,'' Ewing said. ''Maybe it's a concomitant of colonial life. I'll answer you with equal bluntness: there's no outworld colony league, and I'm not on Earth with the remotest intention of establishing a dominion here.''

''Then why *are* you here?''

He scowled impatiently. ''I explained all that to our friend Firnik this morning, only a few minutes after I had entered the spaceport terminal. I told him that Corwin's in danger of an alien invasion, and that I had come to Earth seeking help.''

''Yes, you told him that. And you expected him to *believe* that story?''

Exasperated, Ewing howled, ''Dammit, why not? It's the *truth!*''

''That any intelligent person would cross fifty light-years simply to ask military aid from the weakest and most helpless planet in the universe? You can think up better lies than that one,'' she said mockingly.

He stared at her. ''We're an isolated planet,'' he

said in a quiet but intense voice. "We didn't know anything at all about the current state of Earth's culture. We *thought* Earth could help us. I came on a fool's errand, and I'm going home again tomorrow, a sadder and wiser man. Right now I'm tired and I want to get some sleep. Will you please leave?"

She rose without warning and took a seat next to him on the bed. "All right," she said in a husky but surprisingly soft voice. "I'll tell Firnik you're here for the reasons you say you are."

Her words might have startled him, but he was expecting them. It was a gambit designed to keep him off guard. The Sirian methods were crude ones.

"Thanks," he said sarcastically. "Your faith in me is heart-warming."

She moved closer to him. "Why don't you have a drink with me? I'm not *all* Sirian Consulate, you know. I do have an after-hours personality too, much as you may find it hard to believe."

He sensed her warmth against his body. She reached out, poured him a drink, and forced the glass into his reluctant hand. Ewing wondered whether Firnik were watching this at the other end of the spy beam.

Her hands caressed his shoulders, massaging gently. Ewing looked down at her pityingly. Her eyes were closed, her lips moist, slightly parted. Her breathing was irregular. *Maybe she isn't faking*, he thought. But even so, he wasn't interested.

He moved suddenly away from her, and she nearly lost her balance. Her eyes opened wide; for an instant naked hatred blazed in them, but she recovered quickly and assumed a pose of hurt innocence.

"Why did you do that? Don't you like me?"

Ewing smiled coldly. "I find you amusing. But I don't like to make love in front of a spy beam."

Her eyes narrowed; her lips curled downward in a momentary scowl, and then she laughed—derisive, silver laughter. "You think that was an *act?* That I was doing all that for the greater glory of the Fatherland?"

He nodded. "Yes."

She slapped him. It was utterly predicatable; he had been waiting for it from the moment the affirmative word left his lips. The blow had an astonishing amount of force behind it; Byra Clork packed quite a wallop, Ewing decided ruefully. He wondered if he had misjudged her intentions; it made no difference, really.

"Will you leave now?" he asked.

"I might as well," she muttered bitterly. She glowered at him. "If you're a sample of Corwinite manhood, I'm glad they don't come here more often than once every five hundred years. Machine! Robot!"

"Are you quite through?"

She picked up a light wrap that had been on the back of the chair, and arranged it around her shoulders. Ewing made no move to help her. He waited impassively, arms folded.

"You're incredible," she said, half scornfully, half otherwise. She paused; then a light entered her eyes. "Will you have a drink with me, at least, before I go?"

She was being crafty, he thought, but clumsily so. She had offered him the drink so many times in the past half hour that he would be a fool not to suspect it of being drugged. He could be crafty too.

"All right," he said. "I'll have a drink."

He picked up the glass she had poured for him, and handed her the half-full glass that she had held—untasted—throughout the time. He looked expectantly at her.

"What are you waiting for?" she asked.

"Waiting for you to take a drink first," he told her.

"Still full of strange suspicions, eh?" She lifted her glass and plainly took a deep draft. Then she handed her glass to Ewing, took his, and sipped it also.

"There," she said, exhaling briefly. "I'm still alive. No deadly poison lurks in either glass. Believe me?"

He smiled. "This time, if no other."

Still smiling, he lifted the glass. The liquor was warm and potent; he felt it course down his throat. A moment later, his legs wobbled.

He struggled to stay up. The room swirled around him; he saw her triumphant, grinning face above him, circling madly as if in orbit. He dropped to his knees and clung to the carpeting for support.

"It *was* drugged," he said.

"Of course. It was a drug that doesn't happen to react on Sirian metabolisms. We weren't sure whether it worked on Corwinites; now we know."

He gripped the carpet. The room rocked wildy. He felt sick, and bitterly angry at himself for having let her trick him into taking the drink. He fought for consciousness. He was unable to rise.

Still conscious, he heard the door of his room open. He did not look up. He heard Byra say, "Did you watch it the whole time?"

"We did." The voice was Firnik's. "You still think he's holding back?"

"I'm sure of it," Byra said. Her tone was vidictive. "He'll need some interrogation before he starts talking."

"We'll take care of that," Firnik said. He barked an order in a language incomprehensible to Ewing. The Corwinite tried to cry for help, but all that escaped his quivering lips was a thin, whining moan.

"He's still fighting the drug," he heard Byra say. "It ought to knock him out any minute."

Shimmering waves of pain beat at him. He lost his grip on the carpet and went toppling over to one side. He felt strong hands gripping him under the arms and lifting him to his feet, but his eyes would not focus any longer. He writhed feebly and was still. Darkness closed in about him.

SEVEN

COLDNESS clung to him. He lay perfectly still, feeling the sharp cold all about him. His hands were pinned to his sides. His legs were likewise pinioned. And all about him was the cold, chilling his skin, numbing his brain, freezing his body.

He made no attempt to move and scarcely any even to think. He was content to lie back here in the darkness and wait. He believed he was on the ship heading homeward to Corwin.

He was wrong. The sound of voices far above him penetrated his consciousness, and he stirred uncertainly, knowing there could be no voices aboard the ship. It was a one-man ship. There was no room for anyone else.

The voices continued––rumbling low murmurs that tickled his auditory nerves without resolving themselves into sequences of intelligible words. Ewing moved about restlessly. Where could he be? Who could be making these blurred, fuzzy sounds?

He strained toward consciousness now; he fought to open his eyes. A cloud of haze obscured his vision. He sat up, feeling stiff muscles protest as he pushed his way up. His eyes opened, closed again immediately as a glare of light exploded in them, and gradually opened again. His head cleared. He adjusted to the light.

His mouth tasted sour; his tongue seemed to be covered with a thick fuzz. His eyes stung. His head hurt, and there was a leaden emptiness in his stomach.

"We've been waiting more than two days for you to wake up, Ewing," said a familiar voice. "That stuff Byra gave you must have really been potent."

He broke through the fog that hazed his mind and looked around. He was in a large room with triangular, opaqued windows. Around him, where he lay on some sort of makeshift cot, were four figures: Rollun Firnik, Byra Clork, and two swarthy Sirians whom he did not know.

"Where am I?" he demanded.

Firnik said, "You're in the lowest level of the Consulate building. We brought you here early Sixday morning. This is Oneday. You've been asleep."

"Drugged is a better word," Ewing said bleakly. He sat up and swung his legs over the side of the cot. Immediately, one of the unknown Sirians stepped forward, put one hand on his chest, grabbed his ankles in his other hand, and heaved him back to the cot, Ewing started to rise again; this time he drew a stinging backhand slap that split his lower lip and sent a dribble of blood down his chin.

Ewing rubbed the moist spot tenderly. Then he came halfway to a sitting position. "What right do you have to keep me here? I'm a citizen of Corwin. I have my rights."

Firnik chuckled. "Corwin's fifty light-years away. Right now you're on Earth. The only rights you have are the ones I say you have."

Angrily, Ewing attempted to spring to his feet. "I demand that you release me! I—"

"Hit him," Firnik said tonelessly.

Again the barrel-bodied Sirian moved forward silently and slapped him—in the same place. Ewing felt the cut on his lip widen, and this time one of his lower teeth abraded the delicate inner surface of his lip as well. He did not make any further attempts to rise.

"Now, then," Firnik said in a conversational voice. "If you're quite sure you'll refrain from causing any more trouble, we can begin. You know Miss Clork, I think."

Ewing nodded.

"And these gentlemen here"—Firnik indicated the two silent Sirians—"are Sergeant Drayl and Lieutenant Thirsk of the City of Valloin Police. I want you to realize that there'll be no need for you to try to call the police, since we have two of their finest men with us today."

"Police? Aren't they from Sirius IV?"

"Naturally." Firnik's eyes narrowed. "Sirians make the best policemen. More than half of the local police are natives of my planet."

Ewing considered that silently. The hotels, the police—what else? The Sirians would not need a bloody coup to establish their power officially; they had already taken control of Earth by default, with the full consent, if not approval, of the Terrestrials. When the time came, all the Sirians needed to do was to give Governor-General Mellis formal notice that he was relieved of his duties, and Earth would pass officially into Sirian possession.

The Corwinite let his gaze roam uneasily around the room. Unfamiliar-looking machines stood in the corners of the room. *The latest in torture devices*, he thought. He looked at Firnik.

"What do you want with me?"

The Sirian folded his thick arms and said, "Information. You've been very stubborn, Ewing."

"I've been telling the truth. What do you want me to do—make something up to please you?"

"You're aware that the government of Sirius IV is soon to extend a protectorate to Earth," Firnik said. "You fail to realize that this step is being done for the mother world's own good, to protect it in its declining days against possible depredations from hostile worlds in this system. I'm not talking about hypothetical invaders from other galaxies."

"Hypothetical? But—"

"Quiet. Let me finish. You, representing Corwin and possibly some of the other distant colonies, have come to Earth to verify the rumor that such a protectorate is about to be created. The worlds you represent have arrived at the totally false conclusion that there is something malevolent about our attitude toward Earth—that we have so-called imperialistic 'designs' on Earth. You fail to understand the altruistic motives behind our decision to relieve the Terrestrials of the tiresome burden of governing themselves. And so your planet has sent you here as a sort of spy, to determine in actuality what the relationship between Sirius IV and Earth is, and to make the necessary arrangements with the Terrestrials to defend Earth against us. To this end you've already conferred with Governor-General Mellis, and you have an appointment to visit one Myreck, a dangerous radical and potential revolutionary. Why do you insist on denying this?''

''Because you're talking idiotic gibberish! I'm no spy! I'm—''

The side of Sergeant Drayl's stiffened hand descended on Ewing at the point where his neck joined his shoulder. He gagged but retained control over himself. His clavicle began to throb.

''You've told both Miss Clork and myself,'' Firnik said, ''that your purpose in coming to Earth was to seek Terrestrial aid against an alleged invasion of non-human beings from beyond the borders of this galaxy. It's such a transparently false story that it makes you and your planet look utterly pitiful.''

''It happens to be true,'' Ewing said doggedly.

Firnik snorted. ''True? There is no such invasion!''

''I've seen photos of Barnholt—''

The barrage of punches that resulted nearly collapsed him. He compelled himself to cling to consciousness, but he was dizzy with pain. A red haze swirled around his head, it seemed.

''You pose a grave threat to joint Sirian-Terrestrial security,'' Firnik said sonorously. ''We must have the truth from you, so we can guide our actions accordingly.''

You've had the truth, Ewing said silently. He did not speak it aloud; that would only be inviting a blow.

''We have means of interrogation,'' Firnik went

on. "Most of them, unfortunately, involve serious demolition of the personality. We are not anxious to damage you; you would be more useful to us with your mind intact."

Ewing stared blankly at him—and at Byra, standing wordlessly at his side.

"What do you want me to tell you?" he asked.

"Details of the Corwinite plans. Full information on the essence of your interview with Governor-General Mellis. Information on possible belligerent intentions on the part of other colony worlds."

"I've told you all I can tell you," Ewing said wearily. "Anything else will be lies."

Firnik shrugged. "We have time. The present mode of interrogation will continue until either some response is forthcoming or we see that your defenses are too strong. After that"—he indicated the hooded machines in the corners of the room—"other means will be necessary."

Ewing smiled faintly despite the pain and the growing stiffness of his lips. He thought for a flickering moment of his wife Laira, his son Blade, and all the others on Corwin, waiting hopefully for him to return with good news. And instead of a triumphant return bearing tidings of aid, he faced torture, maiming, possible death at the hands of Sirians who refused to believe the truth.

Well, they would find out the truth soon enough, he thought blackly. After the normal means of interrogation were shown to be useless, when they had put into use the mind-pick and the brain-burner and the other cheerful devices waiting in the shadowy corners for him. They would turn his mind inside out and reveal its inmost depths, and then they would find he had been telling the truth.

Perhaps then they would begin to worry about the Klodni. Ewing did not care. Corwin was lost to the aliens whether he returned or not, and possibly it was better to die now than to live to see his planet's doom.

He looked up at the Sirian's cold, heavy features with something like pity. "Go ahead," he said gently. "Start interrogating. You're in for a surprise."

EIGHT

A TIMELESS stretch of blurred minutes, hours, perhaps even days slipped by. They had taken away Ewing's watch, along with his wallet and other personal belongings, and so he had no way of perceiving the passage of time. After the first few hours, he hardly cared.

The questioning went on round-the-clock. Usually it was Firnik who stood above him and urged him to confess, while Drayl or Thirsk hovered at one side, punching him from time to time. Sometimes it was Byra who interrogated him, in a flat metallic voice that might have issued from the throat of a robot.

He felt his resources weakening. His answers became mere hazy mumbles, and when they became too incoherent they dashed cold water in his face to revive him.

His tormentors were showing signs of weakening too. Firnik looked red-eyed from the strain; occasionally his voice took on a ragged, rasping quality.

He pleaded with Ewing, cajoled him to end his stubborness and yield the information.

Once, when Ewing had muttered for the millionth time, "I told you the truth the first time," Byra looked sharply at Firnik and said, "Maybe he's sincere. Maybe we're making a mistake. How long can we keep this up?"

"Shut up!" Firnik blazed. He wheeled on the girl and sent her spinning to the floor with a solid slap. A moment later, ignoring Ewing, he picked her up and muttered an apology. "We'll have to use the mind-pick," he said. "We are getting nowhere this way."

Vaguely, Ewing heard something being rolled over the stone floor toward his cot. He did not look up. He heard Byra saying, "There'll be nothing left of him when the pick's through digging through his mind."

"I can't help that, Byra. We have to know. Drayl, have you accounted for the power drain?"

"Yes."

"Then lower the helmet and attach the electrodes."

Ewing opened his eyes and saw a complex instrument by the side of his cot; its myriad dials and meters looked like fierce eyes to him. A gleaming copper helmet hung from a jointed neck. Sergeant Drayl was moving the helmet toward him, lowering it over his head. Clamps within the helmet gripped his skull gently.

He felt metal things being attached to his wrists. He remained perfectly still. He felt no fear, only a dull sensation of relief that the interrogation was at last approaching its conclusion.

"It's ready to function, sir," came Drayl's voice.

"Very well." Firnik sounded a little tense. "Ewing, can you hear me?"

"Yes," he said after some moment's silence.

"Good. You have your last chance. Why did the Free World of Corwin decide to send you to Earth?"

"Because of the Klodni," Ewing began wearily. "They came out of Andromeda and—"

Firnik cut him off: "Enough! I'm turning on the pick."

Under the helmet, Ewing relaxed, waiting for the numbing thrust. A second passed, and another. *Is this what it's like?* he wondered dully.

He heard Firnik's voice, in sudden alarm: "Who are you? How did you get in here?"

"Never mind that." It was a strange voice, firm and commanding. "Get away from that machine, Firnik. I've got a stunner here, and I'm itching to use it on you. Over there, against the wall. You too, Byra. Drayl, unclamp his wrists and get that helmet off him."

Ewing felt the machinery lifting away from him. He blinked, looked around the room without comprehending. A tall figure stood near the door, holding a glittering little gun firmly fixed on the Sirians. He wore a face mask, a golden sheath that effectively concealed his features.

The newcomer crossed the room, coming to the side of Ewing's cot, and lifted him with one hand while keeping the stunner trained on the baffled Sirians. Ewing was too weak to stand on his own power; he wobbled uncertainly, but the stranger held him up.

"Get on the phone, Firnik, and make sure you

keep that vision off. Call the Consulate guard and tell him that the prisoner is being remanded to custody and will leave the building. The stunner's on full intensity now. One phony word and I'll freeze your brains for good."

Ewing felt like a figure in a dream. Cradled against his rescuer's side, he watched uncomprehendingly as a bitterly angry Firnik phoned upstairs and relayed the stranger's message.

"All right, now," the stranger said. "I'm leaving the building and I'm taking Ewing with me. But first"—he made an adjustment on the gun he was carrying—"I think it's wise to take precautions. This ought to keep you out of circulation for a couple of hours, at least."

Firnik made a strangled sound deep in his throat and leaped forward, arms clawing for the masked stranger. The stranger fired once; a blue stream of radiance came noiselessly from the muzzle of the gun, and Firnik froze in his tracks, his face locked in an expression of rage. Calmly the stranger directed his fire around the room until Byra, Drayl, and Thirsk were just three more statues.

Ewing felt the stranger tighten his hold on him. He tried to share the burden by moving himself, but his feet refused to support him.

Half-dragged, half-stumbling, he let himself be carried from the room and into a lift. He sensed upward motion. The lift stopped; he was moving forward. Gray waves of pain shuddered through him. He longed to stop where he was and go to sleep, but the inexorable pressure of the stranger's arm carried him along.

Fresh air reached his nostrils. He coughed. He had become accustomed to the foul staleness of the room that had been his prison.

Through half-open eyes he watched the companion hail a cab; he was pushed inside, and heard the voice say, "Take us to the Grand Valloin Hotel, please."

"Looks like your friend's really been on a binge," the driver said. "Don't remember the last time I saw a man looking so used up."

Why is he taking me back to the hotel? Ewing wondered. *Firnik has spy beams planted there.*

The gentle motion of the cab was soothing; after a few moments he dropped off to sleep. He woke later, once again being supported by the stranger. Upward. Into a corridor. Standing in front of a door.

The door opened. They went in.

It was his room at the hotel.

He staggered forward and fell face-first on the bed. He was aware of the stranger's motions as he undressed him, washed his face, applied depilatory to his beard.

"I want to go to sleep," he said.

"Soon. Soon."

He was carried into the adjoining room and held under the shower until the ion-beam had peeled away the grime. Then, at last, he was allowed to sleep. The bedsheets were warm and womblike; he nestled in them gratefully, letting his tortured body relax, letting sleep sweep up over him and engulf him.

Vaguely he heard the door close behind him. He slept.

He woke some time later, his body stiff and sore in

a hundred places. He tolled over in the bed, clamping a hand to his forehead to stop the throbbing back of his eyes.

What happened to me?

Memory came flooding back. He recalled finding Byra in his room, taking the drugged liquor, being carried off to the Sirian Consulate. Blurred days of endless torment, interrogation, a mind-pick machine lowered over his unresisting head—

Sudden resuce from an unknown source. Sleep. His memories ended there.

Achingly, he crawled from the bed and switched on the room telestat, dialed the news channel. The autotyper rattled, and a news report began to unwind from the machine:

Fourday, 13th Fifthmonth, 3806. The office of Governor-General Mellis announced today that plans are continuing for construction of the Gerd River Dam, despite Sirian objections that the proposed power plant project would interfere with the power rights granted them under the Treaty of 3804. The Governor-General declared—

Ewing did not care what the Governor-General had declared. His sole purpose in turning on the telestat had been to find out the date.

Fourday, the thirteenth of Fifthmonth, He calculated backward. He had had his interview with Mellis the previous Fiveday evening; that had been the seventh of Fifthmonth. On Fiveday night—Sixday morning, actually—he had been kidnapped by Firnik.

Two days later, on Oneday, he had awakened and the torture began. Oneday, Twoday, Threeday—and this was Fourday. The torture had lasted no more than two days, then. The stranger had rescued him either on Twoday or Threeday, and he had slept through until today.

He remembered something else: he had made his appointment with Myreck for Fournight. Tonight.

The house phone chimed.

Ewing debated answering it for a moment; it chimed again more insistently, and he switched it on. The robotic voice said, "There is a call for you, Mr. Ewing. Shall we put it through?"

"Who's it from?" he asked cautiously.

"The party did not say."

He considered. "Okay," he said finally. "Put whoever it is on."

Moments later the screen brightened and Ewing saw the hairless image of Scholar Myreck staring solicitously at him. "Have I disturbed you?" Myreck asked.

"Not at all," Ewing said. "I was just thinking about you. We had an appointment for tonight, didn't we?"

"Ah—yes. But I have just received an anonymous call telling me you have had a rather unfortunate experience. I was just wondering if I could be of any service to you in alleviating your pain."

Ewing remembered the miraculous massage Myreck had given him earlier. He also considered the fact that the hotel he was in belonged to Firnik, and no doubt the Sirian would be fully recuperated from his stunning soon and out looking for him. It was unwise to remain in the hotel any longer.

He smiled. "I'd be very grateful if you would be. You said you'd arrange to pick me up, didn't you?"

"Yes. We will be there in a few minutes."

NINE

IT TOOK only eleven minutes from the time Ewing broke contact to the moment when Myreck rang up from the hotel lobby to announce that he had arrived. Ewing took the rear liftshaft down, and moved cautiously through the vast lobby toward the energitron concession, which was where the Scholar had arranged to meet him.

A group of Earthers waited there for him. He recognized Myreck, and also the uniped he had seen the first morning at the terminal. The other two were equally grotesque in appearance. In a pitiful quest for individuality, they had given themselves up to the surgeon's knife. One had a row of emerald-cut diamonds mounted crest-fashion in a bare swath cut down the center of his scalp; the inset jewels extended past his forehead, ending with one small gem at the bridge of his nose. The fourth had no lips, and a series of blue cicatrices incised in parallel lines on his jaws. For the first time Ewing felt no distaste at the sight of these altered Earthmen, partly because he was so exhausted physically and partly because he was growing accustomed to the sight of them.

Myreck said, "The car is outside."

It was a stubby three-color model which seemed not to have any windows whatever. Ewing wondered whether it was robocontrolled, or whether the driver drove by guesswork. He found out quickly enough when he got in, and discovered that the dome of green plastic that roofed the car was actually a sheet of some one-way viewing material; far from having no access to the outside world, the driver and passengers had a totally unobstructed view in all directions, and unlimited privacy as well.

Myreck drove; or rather, he put the car in motion, and then guided it by deft occasional wrist-flicks on the directional control. They turned south, away from the spaceport, and glided along a broad highway for nearly eight miles, turning eastward sharply into what seemed like a surburban district. Ewing slumped tiredly in his corner of the car, now and then peering out at the neat, even rows of houses, each one surmounted by its own glittering privacy shield.

At last they pulled up at the side of the road. Ewing was startled to see nothing before them but an empty lot. There were some houses further down the street, and plenty of parking space in front of them; why had Myreck chosen to park here?

Puzzled, he got out. Myreck stared cautiously in all directions, then took a key made of some luminous yellow metal from his pocket and advanced toward the empty lot, saying, "Welcome to the home of the College of Abstract Science."

"Where?"

Myreck pointed to the lot. "Here, of course."

Ewing squinted; something was wrong about the air above the lot. It had a curious pinkish tinge, and seemed to be shimmering, as if heat-waves were rising from the neatly tended grass.

Myreck held his key in front of him, stepped into the lot and groped briefly in mid-air, as if searching for an invisible keyhole. And indeed he seemed to find it; the key vanished for three-quarters of its length.

A building appeared.

It was a glistening pink dome, much like the other houses in the neighborhood; but it had a curious impermanence about it. It seemed to be fashioned of dream-stuff. The lipless Earther grasped him firmly by the arm and pushed him forward, into the house. The street outside disappeared.

"That's a neat trick," Ewing said. "How do you work it?"

Myreck smiled. "The house is three microseconds out of phase with the rest of the street. It always exists just a fraction of an instant in Absolute Past, not enough to cause serious temporal disturbance but enough to conceal it from our many enemies."

Goggle-eyed, Ewing said, "You have temporal control?"

The Earther nodded. "The least abstract of our sciences. A necessary defense."

Ewing felt stunned. Gazing at the diminutive Earther with new-found respect, he thought, *This is incredible!* Temporal control had long been deemed theoretically possible, ever since the publication of Blackmuir's equations more than a thousand years before. But Corwin had had little opportunity for temporal research, and such that had been done had seemed to imply that Blackmuir figures were either incorrect or else technologically un-implementable. And for these overdecorated Earthers to have developed them! Unbelievable!

He stared through a window at the quiet street outside. In Absolute Time, he knew, the scene he was observing was three microseconds in the future, but the interval was so minute that for all practical purposes it made no difference to the occupants of the house. It made a great difference to anyone outside who wanted to enter illegally, though; there was no way to enter a house that did not exist in present time.

"This must involve an enormous power-drain," Ewing said.

"On the contrary. The entire operation needs no more than a thousand watts to sustain itself. Our generator supplies fifteen-amp current. It's astonishingly inexpensive, though we never could have met the power demands had we tried to project the house an equivalent distance into the *future*. But there's time to talk of all this later. You must be exhausted. Come."

Ewing was led into a comfortably-furnished salon lined with microreels and music disks. Plans were pinwheeling in his head, nearly enough to make him forget the fatigue that overwhelmed his body. *If these Earthers have temporal control,* he thought, *and if I can induce them to part with their device or its plans. . .*

It's pretty far-fetched. But we need something far-fetched to save us now. It might work.

Myreck said, "Will you sit here?"

Ewing climbed into a relaxing lounger. The Earther dialed him a drink and slipped a music disk into the player. Vigorous music filled the room: foursquare harmonics, simple and yet ruggedly powerful. He liked the sort of sound it made—a direct emotional appeal.

"What music is that?"

"Beethoven," Myreck said. "One of our ancients. Would you like me to relax you?"

"Please."

Ewing felt Myreck's hands at the base of his skull once again. He waited. Myreck's hands probed the sides of his neck, lifted, jabbed down sharply. For one brief moment Ewing felt all sensation leave his body; then physical awareness returned, but without consciousness of the pain.

"That feels wonderful," he said. "It's as if Firnik never worked me over at all, except for these bruises I have as souvenirs."

"They'll vanish shortly. Somatic manifestations usually do once the pain-source is removed."

He leaned back, exulting in the sensation of feeling no pain as if he had spent all his life, and not merely the past three of four days, in a state of hellish physical discomfort. The music was fascinating, and the drink he held warmed him. It was comforting to know that somewhere in the city of Valloin was a sanctuary where he was free from Firnik for as long as he chose.

The Earthers were filing in now—eleven or twelve of them, shy little men with curious artificial deformities of diverse sorts. Myreck said, "There are the members of the College currently in residence. Others are doing research elsewhere. I don't know what sort of colleges you have on Corwin, but ours is the one only in the most ancient sense of the world. We draw no distinctions between master and pupil here. We all learn equally from one another.

"I see. And which of you developed the temporal control system?"

"Oh, none of us did that. Powlis was responsible, a hundred years ago. We've simply maintained the apparatus and modified it."

"A hundred years?" Ewing was appalled. "It's a hundred years since the art was discovered and you're still lurking in holes and corners, letting the Sirians push you out of control of your own planet?"

Ewing realized he had spoken too strongly. The Earthers looked abashed; some of them were almost at the verge of tears. *They're like children,* he thought wonderingly.

"I'm sorry," he said.

A slim Earther with surgically-augmented shoulders said, "Is it true that your world is under attack by alien beings from a far galaxy?"

"Yes. We expect attack in ten years."

"And will you be able to defeat them?"

Ewing shrugged. "We'll try. They've conquered the first four worlds they've attacked, including two that were considerably stronger than we are. We don't have much hope of winning. But we'll try."

Sadly Myreck said, "We had been wondering if it would be possible for us to leave Earth and emigrate to your world soon. But if you face destruction. . ." He let his voice trail off.

"Emigrate to Corwin? Why would you do that?"

"The Sirians soon will rule here. They will put us to work for them, or else kill us. We're safe as long as we remain in this building—but we must go out from time to time."

"You have temporal control. You could duck back into yesterday to avoid pursuit."

Myreck shook his head. "Paradoxes are caused. Multiplication of personality. We fear these things, and we would hesitate to bring them about."

Shrugging, Ewing said, "You have to take chances. Caution is healthy only when not carried to excess."

"We had hoped," said a dreamy-eyed Earther sitting in the corner, "that we could arrange with you for a passage to Corwin. On the ship you came on, possibly."

"It was a one-man ship."

Disappointment was evident. "In that case, perhaps you could send a larger ship for us. We have none, you see. Earth stopped building ships two centuries ago, and gradually most of the ones we had were either sold or fell into disuse. The Sirians now control such industries on Earth, and refuse to let us have ships. So the galaxy we once roamed is closed to us."

Ewing wished there were some way he could help these futile, likable little dreamers. But no solutions presented themselves. "Corwin has very few ships itself," he said. "Less than a dozen capable of making an interstellar journey with any reasonable number of passengers. And any ships we might have would certainly be requisitioned by the military for use in the coming war against the Klodni. I don't see any way we could manage it. Besides," he added, "even if I left Earth tomorrow, I wouldn't be back on Corwin for nearly a year. And it would take another year for me to return to Earth with a ship for you. Do you think you could hold out against the Sirians that long?"

"Possibly," Myreck said, but he sounded doubtful. There was silence a moment. Then the Scholar said, "Please understand that we would be prepared to pay for our passage. Not in money, perhaps, but in service. Possibly we are in command of certain scientific techniques not yet developed on your world. In that case you might find our emigration quite valuable."

Ewing considered that. Certainly the Earthers had plenty to offer—the temporal-control device, foremost among them. But he could easily picture the scene upon his return to Corwin, as he tried to get the Council to approve use of a major interstellar freighter to bring refugee scientists from the Earth that had failed to help them. It would never work. If they only had some super-weapon—

But, of course, if they had a super-weapon they would have no need of fleeing the Sirians. Round and round, with no solution.

He moistened his lips. "Perhaps I can think of something," he said. "The cause isn't quite hopeless yet. But meanwhile—"

Myreck's eyes brightened. "Yes?"

"I'm quite curious about your temporal-displacement equipment. Would it be possible for me to examine it?"

Myreck exchanged what seemed like a dubious glance with several of his comrades. After a moment's hesitation he returned his attention to Ewing and said, in a slightly shaky voice, "I don't see why not."

They don't fully trust me, Ewing thought. *They're half afraid of the bold, vigorous man from the stars. Well, I don't blame them.*

Myreck rose and beckoned to Ewing. "Come this way. The laboratory is downstairs."

Ewing followed, and the other Earthers tagged along behind. They proceeded down a winding staircase into a room below, brightly lit with radiance streaming from every molecule of the walls and floor. In the center of the room stood a masssive block of machinery, vaguely helical in structure, with an enormous pendulum held in suspension in its center. A platform stood at one side. Elsewhere in the room were metering devices and less identifiable types of scientific equipment.

"This is not the main machine," Myreck said. "In the deepest level of the building we keep the big generator that holds us out of time-phase with relation to the outside world. I could show it to you, but this machine is considerably more interesting."

"What does this one do?"

"It effects direct temporal transfer on a small-scale level. The theory behind it is complex, but the basic notion is extraordinarily simple. You see—"

"Just a moment," Ewing said, interrupting. An idea had struck him which was almost physically staggering in its impact. "Tell me: this machine could send a person into the immediate Absolute Past, couldn't it?"

Myreck frowned. "Why, yes. Yes. But we could never run the risk of—"

Again Ewing did not let the Earther finish his

statement. "This I find very interesting," he broke in. He moistened his suddenly dry lips. "Would you say it was theoretically possible to send—say, me—back in time to—oh, about Twoday evening of this week?"

"It could be done, yes," Myreck admitted.

A pulse pounded thunderously in Ewing's skull. His limbs felt cold and his fingers seemed to be quivering. But he fought down the feeling of fear. Obviously, the journey had been taken once, and successfully. He would take it again.

"Very well, then. I request a demonstration of the machine. Send me back to Twoday evening."

"But—"

"I insist," Ewing said determinedly. He knew now who his strange masked rescuer had been.

TEN

A LOOK of blank horror appeared on Myreck's pale face. His thin lips moved a moment without producing sound. Finally he managed to say, in a hoarse rasp. "You can't be serious. There would be a continuum doubling if you did that. Two Baird Ewings existing conterminously, you see. And—"

"Is there any danger in it?" Ewing asked.

Myreck looked baffled. "We don't know. It's never been done. We've never dared to try it. The consequences might be uncontrollable. A sudden explosion of galactic scope, for all we know."

"I'll risk it," Ewing said. He knew there had been no danger that *first* time. He was certain now that his rescuer had been an earlier Ewing, one who had preceded him through the time-track, reached this point in time, and doubled back to become his rescuer, precisely as he was about to do. His head swam. He refused to let himself dwell on the confusing, paradoxical aspects of the situation.

"I don't see how we could permit such a dangerous thing to take place," Myreck said mildly. "You put us in a most unpleasant position. The risks are too great. We don't dare."

A spanner lay within Ewing's reach. He snatched it up, hefting it ominously, and said, "I'm sorry to have to threaten you, but you'd never be able to follow me if I tried to explain why I have to do this. Either put me back to Twonight or I'll begin smashing things."

Myreck's hands moved in a little dance of fear and frustration. "I'm sure you wouldn't consider such a violent act, Mr. Ewing. We know you're a reasonable man. Surely you wouldn't—"

"Surely I would!" His hands gripped the shaft tightly; sweat rolled down his forehead. He knew that his bluff would not be called, that ultimately they would yield, since they *had* yielded, once—when? When this scene had become played out for the first time. First? Ewing felt cold uneasiness within.

Limply Myreck shook his head up and down. "Very well," the little man said. "We will do as you ask. We have no choice." His face expressed an emotion as close to contempt as was possible for him—a sort of mild, apologetic disdain. "If you will mount this platform, please . . ."

Ewing put the spanner down and suspiciously stepped forward onto the platform. He sensed the oppressive bulk of the machine around and above him. Myreck made painstaking adjustments on a control panel beyond his range of vision, while the other Earthers gathered in a frightened knot to watch the proceedings.

"How do I make the return trip to Fourday?" Ewing asked suddenly.

Myreck shrugged. "By progressing through forward time at a rate of one second per second. We have no way of returning you to this time or place at any accelerated rate." He looked imploringly at Ewing. "I beg you not to force me to do this. We have not fully worked out the logic of time travel yet; we don't understand—"

"Don't worry. I'll be back. Somehow. Sometime."

He smiled with a confidence he did not feel. He was setting foot into the darkest of realms— *yesterday*. He was armed with one comforting thought: that by venturing all, he might possibly save Corwin. By risking nothing, he would lose all.

He waited. He realized he was expecting a crackle of energy, an upwelling flare of some supernatural force that would sweep him backward across the matrix of time, but none of these phenomena materialized. There was merely the gentle murmur of Myreck's voice as he called off equations and made compensations on his control panel; then came a final "Ready," and the Earther's hand reached for the ultimate switch.

"There'll probably be a certain amount of spacial dislocation," Myreck was saying. "I hope for our sakes that you emerge in the open, and not—"

The sentence was never finished. Ewing felt no sensation whatever, but the laboratory and the tense group of Earthers vanished as if blotted out by the hand of the cosmos, and he found himself hovering a foot in the air in the midst of a broad greensward, on a warm, bright afternoon.

The hovering lasted only an instant; he tumbled heavily to the ground, sprawling forward on his hands and knees. He rose hurriedly to his feet. His knee stung for an instant as he straightened up; he glanced down and saw that he had scraped it on a stone in the field, causing a slight abrasion.

From nearby came a childish giggle. A high voice said, "Look at the funny man doing handsprings!"

"Such a remark is impolite," came a stuffy, mechanical-sounding response. "One does not loudly call attention to eccentric behavior of any kind."

Ewing turned and saw a boy of about eight being admonished by a tall robot governess. "But where did the man come from?" the boy persisted. "He just dropped out of the sky, didn't he? Didn't you see?"

"My attention was elsewhere. But people do not drop out of the sky. Not in this day and age in the City of Valloin."

Chuckling to himself, Ewing walked away. It was good to know he was still in the City of Valloin, at any rate; he wondered if the boy was going to continue asking about the man who had dropped from the sky. That governess didn't seem to have any humor circuits. He pitied the boy.

He was in a park; that much was obvious. In the distance he saw a children's playground ,and something that might have been a zoological garden. Concessions sold refreshments nearby. He walked toward the closest of these booths, where a bright-haired young man was purchasing a balloon for a boy at his side from a robot vender.

"Excuse me," he said. "I'm a stranger in Valloin, and I'm afraid I've got myself lost."

The Earther—his hair, a flaming red, had apparently been chemically treated to look even brighter—handed the robot a coin, took the balloon, gave it to the child, and smiled courteously at Ewing. "Can I help you?"

Ewing returned the smile. "I was out for a walk, and I'm afraid I lost my way. I'd like to get back to the Sirian Consulate. That's where I'm staying."

The Earther gaped at him a moment before recovering control. "You *walked* all the way from the Sirian Consulate to Valloin Municipal Park?"

Ewing realized he had made a major blunder. He reddened and tried to cover up for himself: "No—no, not exactly. I know I took a cab part of the way. But I don't remember which way I came, and—well—"

"You could take a cab back, couldn't you?" the young man suggested. "Of course, it's pretty expensive from here. If you want, take the Number Sixty bus as far as Grand Circle, and transfer there for the downtown undertube line. The Oval Line tube will get you to the Consulate if you change at the Three Hundred Seventy-eighth Street station."

Ewing waited patiently for the flow of directions to cease. Finally he said, "I guess I'll take the bus, then. Would it be troubling you too much to show me where I could get it?"

"At the other side of the park, near the big square entrance."

Ewing squinted. "I'm afraid I don't see it. Could we walk over there a little way? I wouldn't want to inconvenience you in any way . . ."

"Perfectly all right."

They left the vendor's booth and started to cross

the park. Halfway toward the big entrance, the Earther stopped. Pointing, he said, "It's right over there. See? You can't miss it."

Ewing nooded. "There's one final thing—"

"Of course."

"I seem to have lost all my money in an unfortunate accident this morning. I lost my wallet, you see. Could you lend me about a hundred credits?"

"A hundred credits! Now, see here, fellow. I don't mind giving travel directions, but a hundred credits is a little out of line! Why it won't cost you more than one credit eighty to get to the Consulate from here."

"I know," Ewing said tightly. "But I need the hundred." He pointed a finger through the fabric of his trouser pocket and said, "There's a stun-gun in this pocket, and my finger's on the stud. Suppose you very quietly hand me a hundred credits in small notes, or I'll be compelled to use the stunner on you. I wouldn't want to do that."

The Earther seemed on the verge of tears. He glanced quickly at the boy with the balloon, playing unconcernedly fifteen feet away, and then jerked his head back to face Ewing. Without speaking, he drew out his billfold and counted out the bills. Ewing took them in equal silence and stored them in the pocket where he had kept his wallet, before Firnik had confiscated it.

"I'm really sorry about having to do this," he told the young Earther. "But I can't stop to explain, and I need the money. Now I'd like you to take the child by the hand and walk slowly toward that big lake over there, without looking back and without calling for help. The stunner is effective at distances of almost five hundred feet, you know."

"Help a stranger and this is what you get," the Earther muttered. "Robbery in broad daylight, in Municipal Park!"

"Go on—move!"

The Earther moved. Ewing watched him long enough to make sure he would keep good faith, then turned and trotted rapidly toward the park entrance. He reached it just as the rounded snout of a Number Sixty bus drew up at the corner. Grinning, Ewing leaped aboard. An immobile robot at the entrance said, "Destination, please?"

"Grand Circle."

"Nothing and sixty, please."

Ewing drew a one-credit note from his pocket, placed it in the receiving slot, and waited. A bell rang; a ticket popped forth, and four copper coins jounced into the change slot. He scooped them up and entered the bus. From the window he glanced at the park and caught sight of the little boy's red balloon; the flame-haired man was next to him, back to the street, staring at the lake. Probably scared stiff, Ewing thought. He felt only momentary regret for what he had done. He needed the money. Firnik had taken all of *his* money, and his rescuer had unaccountably neglected to furnish him with any.

Grand Circle turned out to be just that —a vast circular wheel of a street, with more than fifteen street-spokes radiating outward from it. A monument of some sort stood in a grass plot at the very center of the wheel.

Ewing dismounted from the bus. Spying a robot directing traffic, he said, "Where can I get the downtown undertube line?"

The robot directed him to the undertube station.

He transferred at the Three Hundred Seventy-eighth Street station, as his unfortunate acquaintance had advised, and shortly afterward found himself in the midst of a busy shopping district.

He stood thoughtfully in the middle of the arcade for a moment, nudging his memory for the equipment he would need. A privacy mask and a stun-gun; that seemed to be about all.

A weapons shop sign beckoned to him from the distance. He hurried to it, found it open, and stepped through the curtain of energy that served as its door. The proprietor was a wizened little Earther who smiled humbly at him as he entered.

"May I serve you, sir?"

"You may. I'm interested in buying a stun-gun, if you have one for a good price."

The shopkeeper frowned. "I don't know if we have any stun-guns in stock. Now let me see. . .ah, yes!" He reached below the counter and drew forth a dark-blue plastite box. He touched the seal; the box flew open. "Here you are, sir. A lovely model. Only eight credits."

Ewing took the gun from the little man and examined it. It felt curiously light; he split it open and was surprised to find it was hollow and empty within. He looked up angrily. "Is this a joke? Where's the force chamber?"

"You mean you want a *real* gun, sir? I thought you simply were looking for an ornament to complement that fine suit you wear. But—"

"Never mind that. Do you have one of these that actually functions?"

The shopkeeper looked pale, almost sick. But he

vanished into the back room and reappeared a moment later with a small gun in his hand. "I happen to have one, sir. A Sirian customer of mine ordered it last month and then unfortunately died. I was about to return it, but if you're interested it's yours for ninety credits."

Ninety credits was almost all the money he had. And he wanted to save some to hand over to the rescued man.

"Too much. I'll give you sixty."

"Sir! I—"

"Take sixty," Ewing said. "I'm a personal friend of Vice-Consul Firnik's. See him and he'll make up the difference."

The Earther eyed him meekly and sighed. "Sixty it is," he said. "Shall I wrap it?"

"Never mind about that," Ewing said, pocketing the tiny weapon, case and all, and counting out sixty credits from his slim roll. One item remained. "Do you have privacy masks?"

"Yes, sir. A large assortment."

"Good. Give me a golden one."

With trembling hands the shopkeeper produced one. It fit the memory he had of the other reasonably well. "How much?"

"T-ten credits, sir. For you, eight."

"Take the ten," Ewing said. He folded the mask, smiled grimly at the terrified shopkeeper, and left. Once he was out on the street, he looked up at a big building-clock and saw the time: 1552.

Suddenly he clapped his hand to his forehead in annoyance: he had forgotten to check the most important fact of all! Hastily he darted back into the weapons shop. The proprietor came to attention, lips quivering. "Y-yes."

"All I want is some information," Ewing said. "What day is today?"

"What *day?* Why—why, Twoday, of course. Twoday, the eleventh."

Ewing crowed triumphantly. Twoday on the nose! He burst from the store a second time. Catching the arm of a passerby, he said, "Pardon. Can you direct me to the Sirian Consulate?"

"Two blocks north, turn left. Big building. You can't miss it."

"Thanks," Ewing said.

Two blocks north, turn left. A current of excitement bubbled in his heart.

He began to walk briskly toward the Sirian Consulate, hands in his pockets. One clasped the coolness of the stun-gun, the other rested against the privacy mask.

ELEVEN

EWING had to push his way through a good-sized crowd at the Consulate—Sirians all, each of them bound on some private business of his own. Ewing was surprised that there were so many Sirians in Valloin.

The Consulate was a building of imposing dimensions; evidently one of the newest of Valloin's edifices, its architecture was out of key with that of the surrounding buildings. Clashing planes and tangential faces made the Consulate a startling sight.

Ewing passed through the enormous lobby and turned left to a downramp. He gave only passing thought to the question of how he was going to reach the subterranean dungeon, where at this moment another version of himself was undergoing interrogation. He knew that he had been rescued once, and so it could be repeated.

He made his way down, until a sergeant stationed

at the foot of the last landing said, "Where are you going?"

"To the lowest level. I have to see Vice-Consul Firnik on urgent business."

"Firnik's in conference. He left orders that he wasn't to be disturbed."

"Quite all right. I have special permission. I happen to know he's interrogating a prisoner down below, along with Byra Clork, Sergeant Drayl, and Lieutenant Thirsk. I have vital information for him, and I'll see to it you roast unless I get in there to talk to him."

The sergeant looked doubtful. "Well . . ."

Ewing said, "Look—why don't you go down the hall and check with your immediate superior, if you don't want to take the responsibility yourself? I'll wait here."

The sergeant grinned, pleased to have the burden of decision lifted from his thick shoulders. "Don't go away," he said. "I'll be right back."

"Don't worry," Ewing said.

He watched as the man turned and trudged away. After he had gone three paces, Ewing drew the stunner from his pocket and set it to low intensity. The weapon was palm-size, fashioned from a bit of translucent blue plastic in whose glittering depths could dimly be seen the reaction chamber. Ewing aimed and fired. The sergeant froze.

Quickly, Ewing ran after him, dragged him back to his original position, and swung him around so he seemed to be guarding the approach. Then he ducked around him and headed down toward the lower level.

Another guard, this one in a lieutenant's uniform,

waited there. Ewing said quickly, "The sergeant sent me down this way. Said I could find the Vice-Consul down here. I have an urgent message for him."

"Straight down the passageway, second door on your left," the lieutenant said.

Ewing thanked him and moved on. He paused for a moment outside the indicated door, while donning the privacy mask, and heard sounds from within:

"Good. You have your last chance. Why did the Free World of Corwin decide to send you to Earth?"

"Because of the Klodni," said a weary voice. The accent was a familiar one, a Corwinite one, but the voice was higher in pitch than Ewing would have expected. It was his own voice. A blur of shock swept through him at the sound. "They came out of Andromeda and—"

"Enough!" came the harsh crop of Firnik's voice. "Byra, get ready to record. I'm turning on the pick."

Ewing felt a second ripple of confusion, outside the door. Turning on the pick? Why, then this was the very moment when he had been rescued, two days earlier in his own time-track! In that case, he was now his own predecessor along the time-line, and—he shook his head. Consideration of paradoxes was irrelevant now. Action was called for, not philosophizing.

He put his hand to the door and thrust it open. It gave before his push; he stepped inside, stun-gun gripped tightly in his hand.

The scene was a weird tableau. Firnik, Byra, Drayl, and Thirsk were clustered around a fifth figure who sat limp and unresisting beneath a metal cone. And that fifth figure—

Me!

Firnik looked up in surprise. "Who are you? How did you get in here?"

"Never mind that," Ewing snapped. The scene was unrolling with dreamlike clarity, every phase utterly familiar to him. *I have been here before,* he thought, looking at the limp, tortured body of his earlier self slumped under the mind-pick helmet. "Get away from that machine, Firnik," he snapped. "I've got a stunner here, and I'm itching to use it on you. Over there, against the wall. You, too, Byra. Drayl, unclamp his wrists and get that helmet off him."

The machinery was pulled back, revealing the unshaven, bleary-eyed face of the other Ewing. The man stared in utter lack of comprehension at the masked figure near the door. The masked Ewing felt a tingle of awe at the sight of himself of Twoday, but he forced himself to remain calm. He crossed the room, keeping the gun trained on the Sirians, and lifted the other Ewing to his feet.

Crisply he ordered Firnik to call the Consulate guard upstairs and arrange for his escape. He listened while the Sirian spoke; then, saying, "This ought to keep you out of circulation for a couple of hours, at least," he stunned the four Sirians and dragged his other self from the room, out into the corridor, and into a lift.

It was not until Ewing had reached the street level that he allowed any emotional reaction to manifest itself. Sudden trembling swept over him for an instant as he stepped out of the crowded Sirian Consulate lobby, still wearing the privacy mask, and dragged the semi-conscious other Ewing into the street. The muscles in his legs felt rubbery; his throat was dry. But he had succeeded. He had rescued himself from the interrogators, and the script had followed in every detail that one which seemed "earlier" to him but which was, in reality, not earlier at all.

The script was due to diverge from its "earlier" pattern soon, Ewing realized grimly. But he preferred not to think of the dark necessity that awaited him until the proper time came.

He spied a cab, one of those rare ones not robot-operated, and hailed it. Pushing his companion inside he said, "Take us to the Grand Valloin Hotel, please."

"Looks like your friend's really been on a binge," the driver said. "Don't remember the last time I saw a man looking so used up."

"He's had a rough time of it," Ewing said, watching his other self lapse off into unconsciousness.

It cost five of his remaining eighteen credits to make the trip from the Consulate to the hotel. Quickly, Ewing got his man through the hotel lobby and upstairs into Room 4113. The other—Ewing-sub-two, Ewing was calling him now—immediately toppled face-down onto the bed. Ewing stared curiously at Ewing-sub-two, studying the battered, puffy-eyed face of the man who was himself two days earlier. He set about the job of undressing him, depilating him, cleaning him up. He dragged him into the shower and thrust him under the ion-beam; then, satisfied, he put the exhausted man to bed. Within seconds, he had lost his consciousness.

Ewing took a deep breath. So far the script had

been followed; but here, it had to change.

He realized he had several choices. He could walk out of the hotel room and leave Ewing-sub-two to his own devices, in which case, in the normal flow of events, Ewing-sub-two would awaken, be taken to Myreck's, request to see the time machine, and in due course travel back to this day to become Ewing-sub-one, rescuing a new Ewing-sub-two. But that path left too many unanswered and unanswerable questions. What became of the surplus Ewing-sub-ones? In every swing of the time-cycle, another would be created—to meet what fate? It was hopelessly paradoxical.

But there was a way paradox could be avoided. Ewing thought. A way of breaking the chain of cycles that threated to keep infinite Ewings moving on a treadmill forever. But it took a brave man to make that change.

He stared in the mirror. *Do I dare?* he wondered.

He thought of his wife and child, and of all he had struggled for since coming to Earth. *I'm superfluous,* he thought. The man on the bed was the man in whose hands destiny lay. Ewing-sub-one, the re-scuer, was merely a super-numerary, an extra man, a displaced spoke in the wheel of time.

I have no right to remain alive, Ewing-sub-one admitted to himself. His face, in the mirror, was unquivering, unafraid. He nodded; then, he smiled.

His way was clear. He would have to step aside. But he would merely be stepping aside for himself, and perhaps there would be no sense of discontinuity after all. He nodded in the firm decision.

There was a voicewrite at the room desk; Ewing

switched it on, waited a moment as he arranged his thought, and then began to dictate:

"Twoday afternoon. To my self of an earlier time—to the man I call Ewing-sub-two, from Ewing-sub-one. Read this with great care, indeed memorize it, and then destroy it utterly.

"You have just been snatched from the hands of the interrogators by what seemed to you miraculous intervention. You must believe that your rescuer was none other than yourself, doubling back along his time-track from two days hence. Since I have already lived through the time that will now unfold for you, let me tell you what is scheduled to take place for you, and let me implore you to save our mutual existence by following my instructions exactly.

"It is now Twoday. Your tired body will sleep around the clock, and you will awaken on Fourday. Shortly after awakening, you will be contacted by Scholar Myreck, who will remind you of your appointment with him and will make arrangements with you to take you to his College in the suburbs. You will go. While you are there, they will reveal to you the fact that they are capable of shifting objects in time—indeed, their building itself is displaced by three microseconds to avoid investigation.

"At this point in my own time-track, I compelled them to send me back in time from Fourday to Twoday, and upon arriving here proceeded to carry out your rescue. My purpose in making this trip was to provide you with this information, which *my* rescuer neglected to give me. *Under no conditions are you to make a backward trip in time!* The cycle must end with you.

"When Myreck shows you the machine you are to express interest, but you are not to request a demonstration. This will automatically create a new past in which Ewing-sub-three actually did die under Firnik's interrogation, while you, Ewing sub-two, remain in existence, a free agent ready to continue your current operations. If this phase is not clear to you, read it very carefully.

"As for me, I am no longer needed in the plan of events, and so intend to remove myself from the time-stream upon finishing this note. For your information, I intend to do this by short-circuiting the energitron booth in the lobby while I am inside it, a fact which you can verify upon awakening by checking the telestat records for Twoday, the Eleventh. This action, coupled with your refusal to use Myreck's machine, will put an end to the multiplicity of existing Ewings and leave you as the sole occupant of the stage. Make the most of your opportunities. I know you are capable of handling the task well.

"I wish you luck. You'll need it.

"Yours in—believe me—deepest friendship,

"Ewing-sub-one."

When he had finished the note, Ewing drew it from the machine and read it through three times, slowly. There was no rush now. He folded it, drew from his pocket ten credits—something else his predecessor along the time-track had neglected—and sealed the message and the money in an envelope which he placed on the chair next to the sleeping man's head.

Satisfied, he tiptoed from the room, locking the door behind him, and rode down to the hotel lobby. There was no longer any need for the mask, so he discarded it; he had left the stun-gun upstairs, in case Ewing-sub-two might have need for it.

He picked up a phone in the lobby, dialed Central Communications, and said, "I'd like to send a message to Scholar Myreck, care of College of Abstract Science, General Delivery, City of Valloin Branch Office 86." It was the dummy address Myreck had given him. "The message is, quote: Baird Ewing has been interrogated and severely beaten by your enemies. At present he is asleep in his hotel room. Call him this afternoon and arrange to help him. Unquote. Now, that message is not to be delivered before Fourday, no later than noon. Is that clear?"

The robot operator read the message back, including instructions for delivery, and finished with, "One credit, please."

Ewing dropped coins into the slot until the operator signaled acknowledgement. He nodded in satisfaction; the wheels were fully in motion, now, and he could retire from the scene.

He crossed the lobby to a loitering Earther and said, "Excuse me. Could I trouble you for change of a one-credit bill? I'd like to use the energitron booth and I don't have any coins."

The Earther changed the bill for him; they exchanged a few pleasant words, and then Ewing headed for the booth, satisfied that he had planted his identity. When the explosion came, there would be a witness to say that a tall man had just entered the booth.

He slipped a half-credit coin into the booth's admission slot; the energy curtain that was its entrance went light pink long enough for Ewing to step through, and immediately returned to its glossy black opacity afterward. He found himself facing a beam of warm red light.

The energitron booth was simply a commercial adaptation of the ordinary ion-beam shower; it was a molecular spray that invigorated the body and refreshed the soul, according to the sign outside. Ewing knew it was also a particularly efficient suicide device. A bright enamel strip said.

CAUTION!

The operator is warned not to approach the limit-lines inscribed in the booth or to tamper with the mechanism of the energitron. It is highly delicate and may be dangerous in unskilled hands.

Ewing smiled coldly. His time had come to quit the scene—but the body and the personality of Baird Ewing of Corwin would not be obliterated, merely one superfluous extension of it. With steady hands he reached for the sealed control-box; he smashed it open and twisted the rheostat within sharply upward. The quality of the molecular beam changed; it became fuzzier, and crackled.

At the limit-lines of the booth, he knew an area existed where planes of force existed in delicate imbalance; interposing an arm or a leg in such a place could result in a violent explosion. He moved toward the limit-lines and probed with his hands for the danger area.

A sudden thought struck him: *What about my rescuer?* He had left him out of the calculations completely. But yet another Ewing-one had existed, one who had not left any notes nor stun-guns nor money, and who perhaps had not committed suicide, either. Ewing wondered briefly about him; but then he had no further time for wondering, because a blinding light flashed, and a thunderous wave of force rose from the booth and crushed him in its mighty grip.

TWELVE

EWING WOKE.

He felt groggy, stiff and sore in a hundred places, his forehead throbbing. He rolled over in bed, clamped a hand to his forehead, and hung on.

What happened to me?

Memories drifted back to him a thread at a time. He remembered discovering Byra in his room, drinking the drugged liquor she gave him, being hustled away to the Sirian Consulate. Blurred days of endless torment, interrogation, a mind-pick machine lowered over his unresisting head—

Sudden rescue from an unknown source. Sleep. His memories ended there.

Achingly he crawled from the bed and stared at himself in the mirror. He looked frighteningly haggard. Dark circles ringed his eyes like crayon marks, and the skin of his face hung loose under his chin, stretched tight elsewhere. He looked worse than he had at the moment of awakening, some days before, aboard the ship.

An envelope lay on a chair by the side of the bed. He frowned, picked it up, fingered it. It was sealed and addressed to him. He opened it. Five two-credit notes came fluttering out, and along with them a note. He stacked the banknotes neatly on the bed, unfolded the note, and sat down to read.

Twoday afternoon. To myself of an earlier time —to the man I call Ewing-sub-two, From Ewing-sub-one . . .

Bleary-eyed as he was, he came awake while reading the note. His first reaction was one of anger and incredulity; then he rubbed his chin thoughtfully as he considered certain turns of phrase, certain mannerisms of punctuation. He had a fairly distinctive style of voicewrite dictation. And this was a pretty good copy, or else the real thing.

In which case . . .

He switched on the house phone and said, "What's today's date, please?" There was no fear of ridicule from a robot operator.

"Fourday, the thirteenth of Fifthmonth," came the calm answer.

"Thanks. How can I get access to the telestat reports for Twoday the eleventh?"

"We could connect you with Records," the robot suggested.

"Do that," Ewing said, thinking to himself, *This is foolishness. The note's a hoax.*

He heard the *click-click-click* of shifting relays, and then a new robotic voice said, "Records. How may we serve you?"

"I'm interested in the text of a news item that covers an event which took place Twoday afternoon.

The short-circuiting of an energitron machine in the lobby of the Grand Valloin Hotel.''

Almost instantly the robot said, ''We have your item for you. Shall we read it?''

''Go ahead,'' Ewing said in a rasping voice. ''Read it.''

''Twoday, 11th Fifthmonth, 3806. Explosion of an energitron booth in the lobby of the Grand Valloin Hotel this afternoon took one life, caused an estimated two thousand credits' worth of damage, injured three, and disrupted normal hotel service for nearly two hours. The cause of the explosion is believed to have been a successful suicide attempt.

''No body was recovered from the demolished booth, but witnesses recalled having seen a tall man in street clothes entering the booth moments before the explosion. A check of the hotel registry revealed that no residents were missing. Valloin police indicate they will investigate.''

The robot voice paused and said, ''That's all there is. Do you wish a permanent copy? Should we search the files for subsequent information pertinent to the matter?''

''No,'' Ewing said. ''No, no thanks.'' He severed the contact and sat down heavily on the edge of the bed.

It could still be a prank, of course. He had been asleep several days, long enough for the prankster to hear about the explosion and incorporate the incident retroactively in the note. But Occam's Razor made hash of the hoax theory; there were too many inexplicable circumstances and unmotivated actions involved. Assuming that a prior Ewing had doubled in time to carry out the rescue and leave the note was a vastly simpler hypothesis, granting the one major improbability of time-travel.

There would be one fairly definite proof, though. Ewing found a small blue stun-gun lying on his dresser, and studied it thoughtfully.

According to the note, Scholar Myreck would call him soon after he had awakened.

Very well, Ewing thought, *I'll wait for Myreck to call.*

An hour later he was sitting in a relaxing lounger in a salon in the College of Abstract Science, feeling the pain of Firnik's torture leaving him under the ministrations of Myreck's expert fingers. Music welled around him, fascinating ancient music—Beethoven, Myreck had said. He sipped at his drink.

It was all quite incredible to him: the call from Myreck, the trip across Valloin in the domed car, the miraculous building three microseconds out of phase with the rest of the city, and above all the fact that the note in his room was indubitably true. These Earthers had the secret of time travel, and, though none of them were aware of the fact, they had already sent Baird Ewing back through time at least once from a point along the time-stream that still lay ahead, this afternoon of Fourday.

He realized his responsibility, tremendous already, was even greater now. A man had given up his life for him, and though no actual life had ended; it seemed to Ewing that a part of him he had never known had died. Once again he was sole master of his fate.

The conversation moved smoothly along. The Earthers, alert, curious little men, wanted to know about the Klodni menace, and whether the people of Corwin would be able to defeat them when the attack came. Ewing told them the truth: that they would try, but there was not much hope of success.

And then Myreck introduced a new theme: the possibility of arranging transportation for the members of the College to Corwin, where at least they would be safer than on an Earth dominated by Sirius IV.

It seemed a doubtful proposition to Ewing. He explained to the visibly disappointed Earthers what a vast enterprise it would be to transport them, and how few ships Corwin had available for the purpose. He touched on the necessary delays the negotions would involve.

He saw the hurt looks on their faces; there was no help for it, he thought. Corwin faced destruction; Earth, mere occupation. Corwin needed help more urgently. From which direction, he wondered? From whom?

"I'm sorry," he said. "I just don't see how we can offer you asylum. But it seems to me that you would be in an even worse position on Corwin than you will be here under Sirian rule. The Klodni onslaught will be fierce and destructive; the Sirians will probably keep things much as they are, except you'll pay your taxes to them instead of to Mellis' government."

He felt a depressing cloud of futility settle around him. He had accomplished nothing on Earth, found no possible solution for Corwin's problem, not even succeeded in helping these Earthers. They were caught under the heel of Sirius IV, while Corwin now would have to wait for the coming of the Klodni and the inevitable accompanying murderous conquest.

He had failed. Whatever bold plan had been in the mind of the dead Ewing who had left him the note did not hold a corresponding position in his own mind. Clearly, that Ewing had seen some solution for Corwin, some way in which the planet could be defended against the Klodni. But he had said nothing about it in his note.

Perhaps he had had some experience while traveling back in time, something that might have given him a clue to the resolution of the dilemma. . .

Ewing felt a tempting thought: *Perhaps I should make the trip back in time once again, rescue the Ewing I find there, dictate the note to him once again, and add to it whatever information was missing—*

No. He squelched the idea firmly and totally. Another trip through time was out of the question. He had a chance to end the cycle now, and cut himself loose from Earth. It was the sensible thing to do. Return to Corwin, prepare for the attack, defend his home and country when the time came to do so—that was the only intelligent course of action now. It was futile to continue to search Earth for a nonexistent super-weapon.

Better leave Earth to her sad fate, he thought, *and go back to Corwin.*

The conversation straggled to a dull stop. He and the Earthers had little left to say to each other. Each had appealed to the other for help, and neither was in a position to offer aid.

Myreck said, "Let us change the subject, shall we? This talk of fleeing and destruction depresses me."

"I agree," Ewing said.

The music disk ended. Myreck rose, removed it from the player and popped it back into the file. He said, "We have a fine collection of other Earth ancients. Mozart, Bach, Vurris—"

"I'm afraid I've never heard of any of them," Ewing said. "We only have a few surviving disks of the early Terrestrial composers on Corwin. I've heard them all in the museum." He frowned, trying to remember their names. "Schoenberg . . .and Stravinsky, I think. And Bartok. They belonged to one of the original colonists."

Myreck played Bach—a piece called the Goldberg Variations, for a twangy, not unpleasant-sounding instrument called the harpischord. As he explained it, it operated as a sort of primitive sonomar, the tones being produced by the mechanical plucking of strings.

Several of the Scholars were particularly interested in music old and new, and insisted on expounding their special theories. Ewing, at another time, might have been an eager participant in their discussion; now, he listened out of politeness only, paying little attention to what was said. He was trying to recall the text of the note he had read and destroyed earlier in the day. They would show him their time machine. He was to refuse the demonstration. That would cause the necessary alterations in time past, to fit the design intended by Ewing-sub-one.

Whatever *that* had been, Ewing thought.

The afternoon slipped by. At length Myreck said, "We also have done much work in temporal theory, you know. Our machines are in the lower levels of the building. If you are interested—"

"No!" Ewing said, so suddenly and so harshly it was almost a shout. In a more modulated tone he went on, "I mean—no, thanks. I'll have to beg off on that. It's getting quite late, and I'm sure I'd find the time machines so fascinating I'd overstay my visit."

"But we are anxious to have you spend as much time with us as you can," Myreck protested. "If you want to see the machines—"

"No," Ewing repeated forcefully. "I'm afraid I must leave."

"In that case, we will drive you to your hotel."

This must be the point of divergence, Ewing thought as the Earthers showed him to the door and performed the operations that made it possible to pass back into phase with the world of Fournight the Thirteenth outside. *My predecessor never got back out of this building. He doubled into Twonight instead. The cycle is broken.*

He entered the car, and it pulled away from the street. He looked back, at the empty lot that was not empty.

"Some day you must examine our machines," Myreck said.

"Yes . . . yes, of course," Ewing replied vaguely. "As soon as I've taken care of a few pressing matters."

But tomorrow I'll be on my way back to Corwin, he thought. *I guess I never will see your machines.*

He realized that by his actions this afternoon he had brought a new chain of events into existence; he had reached back into Twoday and, by *not* rescuing Firnik's prisoner, had created a Ewing-sub-three who had been mind-picked by the Sirian and who presumably had died two days before. Thus Firnik believed Ewing was dead, no doubt. He would be surprised tomorrow when a ghost requisitioned the ship in storage at Valloin Spaceport and blasted off for Corwin.

Ewing frowned, trying to work out the intricacies of the problem. Well, it didn't matter, he thought. The step had been taken.

For better or for worse, the time-track had been altered.

THIRTEEN

EWING checked out of the Grand Valloin Hotel that next afternoon. It was a lucky thing, he thought, that the management had awarded him that week's free rent; otherwise, thanks to the kidnaping, he would never have been able to settle up. He had only ten credits, and those were gifts from his phantom rescuer, now dead. The bill came to more than a hundred.

The desk-robot was distantly polite as Ewing signed the forms severing him from relationship with the hotel, waiving right to sue for neglected property, and announcing notification of departure from Valloin. "I hope you have enjoyed your stay in this hotel," the robot said in blurred mechanical tones as Ewing finished.

Ewing eyed the metal creature jaundicedly and said, "Oh, yes. Very much. Very much indeed." He shoved the stack of papers across the marbled desktop and accepted his receipted bill. "You'll have my baggage delivered to the spaceport?" he asked.

"Of course, sir. The voucher guarantees it."

"Thanks," Ewing said.

He strolled through the sumptuous lobby, past the light-fountain, past the relaxing-chairs, past the somewhat battered area of the energitron booth, where robots were busily replastering and repainting the damage. It was nearly as good as new. By the end of the day, there would scarcely be an indication that a man had died violently there only three days before.

He passed several Sirians on his way through the lobby to the front street, but he felt oddly calm all the same. So far as Rollun Firnik and the others were concerned, the Corwinite Baird Ewing had died under torture last Twoday. Anyone resembling him resembled him strictly by coincidence. He walked boldly through the cluster of Sirians and out onto the street level.

It was late afternoon. The street-glow was beginning to come up. A bulletin transmitted via telestat had informed the hotel patrons that eighteen minutes of light rain was scheduled for 1400 that Fiveday, and Ewing had delayed his departure accordingly. Now the streets were fresh and sweet-smelling.

Ewing boarded the limousine that the hotel used for transporting its patrons to and from the nearby spaceport, and looked around for his final glance at the Grand Valloin Hotel. He felt tired and a little sad at leaving Earth; there were so many reminders of past glories here, so many signs of present decay. It had been an eventful day for him, but yet curiously eventless; he was returning to Corwin with nothing concrete gained, nothing learned but the fact that there was no help to be had.

He pondered the time-travel question for a moment. Obviously the Earther machine—along with other paradoxical qualities—was able to create matter where none had existed before. It had drawn from *somewhere* the various Ewing bodies, of which at least two and possibly more had existed simultaneously. And it seemed that once a new body was drawn from the fabric of time, it remained in existence, conterminous with his fellows. Otherwise, Ewing thought, my refusal to go back and carry out the rescue would have snuffed me out. It didn't. It merely ended the life of that "Ewing" in the torture-chamber on Twoday.

"Spaceport," a robot voice announced.

Ewing followed the line into the Departures shed. He noticed there were few Earthers in Departures; only some Sirians and a few non-humanoid aliens were leaving Earth. He joined a line that inched up slowly to a robot clerk.

When it was Ewing's turn, he presented his papers. The robot scanned them quickly.

"You are Baird Ewing of the Free World of Corwin?"

"That's right."

"You arrived on Earth on Fiveday, seventh of Fifthmonth of this year?"

Ewing nodded.

"Your papers are in order. Your ship has been stored in Hangar 107-B. Sign this, please."

It was a permission-grant allowing the spaceport attendants to get his ship from drydock, service it for departure, store his belongings on board, and place the vessel on the blasting field. Ewing read the form through quickly, signed it, and handed it back.

"Please go to Waiting Room Y and remain there until your name is called. Your ship should be ready for you in less than an hour."

Ewing moistened his lips. "Does that mean you'll page me over the public address system?"

"Yes."

The idea of having his name called out, with so many Sirians in the spaceport, did not appeal to him. He said, "I'd prefer not to be paged by name. Can some sort of code word be used?"

The robot hesitated. "Is there some reason—"

"Yes." Ewing's tone was flat. "Suppose you have me paged under the name of . . . ah . . . Blade. That's it. Mr. Blade. All right?"

Doubtfully the robot said, "It's irregular."

"Is there anything in the regulations specifically prohibiting such a pseudonym?"

"No, but—"

"If regulations say nothing about it, how can it be irregular? Blade it is, then."

It was easy to baffle robots. The sleek metal face would probably be contorted in bewilderment, if that were possible. At length the robot assented; Ewing grinned cheerfully at it and made his way to Waiting Room Y.

Waiting Room Y was a majestic vault of a room, with a glittering spangled ceiling a hundred feet above his head, veined with glowing rafters of structual beryllium. Freeform blobs of light, hovering suspended at about the eight-foot level, provided most of the illumination. At one end of the room a vast loud-speaker had been erected; at the other, a screen thirty feet provided changing kaleidoscopic patterns of light for bored waiters.

Ewing stared without interest at the whirling light-patterns for a while. He had found a seat in the corner of the waiting room, where he was not likely to be noticed. There was hardly an Earther in the place. Earthers stayed put, on Earth. And this great spaceport, this monument to an era a thousand years dead, was in use solely for the benefit of tourists from Sirius IV and the alien worlds.

A bubble-headed creature with scaly purple skin passed by, each of its claw-like arms clutching a smaller version of itself. *Mr. XXX from Xfiz V,* Ewing thought bitterly. *Returning from a family outing. He's taken the kiddies to Earth to give them an instructive view of dying civilization.*

The three aliens paused not far from where Ewing sat and exchanged foamy, sibilant sentences. *Now he's telling them to take a good look round,* Ewing thought. *None of this may be here the next time they come.*

For a moment despair overwhelmed him, as he realized once again, that both Earth and Corwin were doomed, and there seemed no way of holding back the inexorable jaws of the pincer. His head drooped forward; he cradled it tiredly with his fingertips.

"Mr. Blade to the departure desk, please. Mr. Blade, please report to the departure desk. Mr. Blade . . ."

Dimly, Ewing remembered that they were paging *him*. He elbowed himself from the seat.

"Mr. Blade to the departure desk, please . . ."

"All right," he murmured. "I'm coming."

He followed a stream of bright violet lights down the center of the waiting room, turned left, and headed for the departure desk. Just as he reached it, the loud-speaker barked once more, *"Mr. Blade to the departure desk . . ."*

"I'm Blade," he said to the robot he had spoken with an hour before. He presented his identity card. The robot scanned it.

"According to this your name is Baird Ewing," the robot announced after some study.

Ewing sighed in exasperation. "Check your memory banks! Sure, my name is Ewing—but I arranged to have you page me under the name of Blade. Remember?"

The robot's optic lenses swiveled agitatedly as the mechanical filtered back through its memory bank. Ewing waited impatiently, fidgeting and shifting his weight from foot to foot. After what seemed to be a fifteen-minute wait the robot brightened again and declared, "The statement is correct. You are Baird Ewing, pseudonym Blade. Your ship is waiting in Blast Area Eleven."

Gratefully, Ewing accepted the glowing identity planchet and made his way through the areaway into the departure track. There he surrendered the planchet to a waiting robot attendant who ferried him across the broad field to his ship.

It stood alone, isolated by the required hundred-meter clearance, a slim, graceful needle, golden-green, still bright in the late-afternoon sunlight. He climbed up the catwalk, sprang the hatch, and entered.

The ship smelled faintly musty after its week in storage. Ewing looked around. Everything seemed in order: the somnotank in which he would sleep during the eleven-month journey back to Corwin, the radio equipment along the opposite wall, the visionplate. He spun the dial on the storage compartment and opened it. His few belongings were aboard. He was ready to leave.

But first, a message.

He set up the contacts on the subetheric generator, preparatory to beaming a message via subspace toward Corwin. He knew that his earlier message, announcing arrival, had not yet arrived; it would ride the subetheric carrier wave for another week yet, before reaching the receptors on his home world.

And, he thought unhappily, the second message, announcing departure, would follow it by only a few days. He twisted the contact dial. The *go-ahead* light came on.

He faced the pickup grid. "Baird Ewing speaking, and I'll be brief. This is my second and final message. I'm returning to Corwin. The mission was an absolute failure—repeat, *absolute failure*. Earth is unable to help us. It faces immediate domination by Terrestrial-descended inhabitants of Sirius IV, and culturally they're in worse shape than we are. Sorry to be delivering bad news. I hope you're all still there when I get back. No reports will follow. I'm signing off right now."

He stared reflectively at the dying lights of the generator a moment, then shook his head and rose. Activating the in-system communicator, he requested and got the central coördination tower of the spaceport.

"This is Baird Ewing, in the one-man ship on Blasting Area Eleven. I plan to depart under automatic control in fifteen minutes. Can I have a time check?"

The inevitable robotic voice replied, "The time now is sixteen fifty-eight and thirteen seconds."

"Good. Can I have clearance for departure at seventeen thirteen and thirteen?"

"Clearance granted," the robot said, after a brief pause.

Grunting acknowledgement, Ewing fed the data to his autopilot and threw the master switch. In fourteen-plus minutes, the ship would blast off from Earth, whether or not he happened to be in the protective tank at the time. But there was no rush; it would take only a moment or two to enter the freeze.

He stripped off his clothes, stored them away, and activated the tap that drew the nutrient bath. The autopilot ticked away; eleven minutes to departure.

So long, Earth.

He climbed into the tank. Now his subliminal instructions took over; he knew the procedure thoroughly. All he had to do was nudge those levers with his feet to enter the state of suspension; needles would jab upward into him and the thermostat would begin to function. At the end of the journey, with the ship in orbit around Corwin, he would automatically be awakened to make the landing manually.

The communicator chimed just as he was about to trip the footlevers. Irritated, Ewing glanced up. What could be the trouble?

"Calling Baird Ewing . . . Calling Baird Ewing . . ."

It was central control. Ewing glanced at the clock. Eight minutes to blast off. And there'd be nothing left of him but a pool of jelly if blasting time caught him still wandering around the ship.

Sourly he climbed from the tank and acknowledged the call. "Ewing here. What is it?"

"An urgent call from the terminal, Mr. Ewing. The party says he must reach you before you blast off."

Ewing considered that. Firnik, pursuing him? Or Byra Clork? No. They had seen him die on Twoday. Myreck? Maybe. Who else could it be? He said, "Very well. Switch over the call."

A new voice said, "Ewing?"

"That's right. Who are you?"

"It doesn't matter just now. Listen—can you come to the spaceport terminal right away?"

The voice sounded tantalizing familiar. Ewing scowled angrily. "No. I can't! My autopilot's on and I'm due for blasting in seven minutes. If you can't tell me who you are, I'm afraid I can't bother to alter flight plans."

Ewing heard a sigh. "I *could* tell you who I am. You wouldn't believe me, that's all. But you mustn't depart yet. Come to the terminal."

"No."

"I warn you," the voice said. "I can take steps to prevent you from blasting off—but it'll be damaging to both of us if I do so. Can't you trust me?"

"I'm not leaving this ship on account of any anonymous warnings," Ewing said hotly. "Tell me who you are. Otherwise I'm going to break contact and enter suspension."

Six minutes to blast.

"All right," came the reluctant reply. "I'll tell

you. My name is Baird Ewing, of Corwin. I'm *you*. Now will you get out of that ship?''

FOURTEEN

WITH TENSE FINGERS Ewing disconnected the autopilot and reversed the suspension unit. He called the control tower and in an unsteady voice told them he was temporarily canceling his blasting plans and was returning to the terminal. He dressed again, and was ready when the robocar came shuttling out across the field to pick him up.

He had arranged to meet the other Ewing in the refreshment room where he had had his first meeting with Rollun Firnik after landing on Earth. A soft conversational hum droned in the background as Ewing entered. His eyes, as if magnetically drawn, fastened on the tall, conservatively-dressed figure at the table near the rear.

He walked over and sat down, without being asked. The man at the table favored him with a smile—cold, precise, the very sort of smile Ewing himself would have used in this situation. Ewing moistened his lips. He felt dizzy.

He said, "I don't know quite where to begin. Who are you?"

"I told you. Yourself. I'm Baird Ewing."

The accent, the tone, the sardonic smile—they all fitted. Ewing felt the room swirl crazily around him. He stared levelly at the mirror image on the other side of the table.

"I thought you were dead," Ewing said. "The note you left me—"

"I didn't leave any notes," the other interrupted immediately.

"Hold on there." It was a conversation taking place in a world of nightmare. Ewing felt as if he were stifling. "You rescued me from Firnik, didn't you?"

The other nodded.

"And you took me to the hotel, put me to bed, and wrote me a note explaining things; you finished off by saying you were going downstairs to blow yourself up in an energitron booth—"

Eyes wide in surprise, the other said, "No, not at all! I took you to the hotel and left. I didn't write any notes, or threaten to commit suicide."

"You didn't leave me money? Or a blaster?"

The man across the table shook his head vehemently. Ewing closed his eyes for a moment. "If you didn't leave me that note, *who did?*"

"Tell me about this note," the other said.

Briefly Ewing summarized the contents of the note as well as he could from memory. The other listened, tapping his finger against the table as each point was made. When Ewing was through, the other remained deep in thought, brow furrowed. Finally he said:

"I see it. There were four of us."

"What?"

"I'll put it slowly: I'm the first one of us to go

118

through all this. It begins with a closed-circle paradox, the way any time distortion would have to: me, in the torture chamber, and a future me coming back to rescue me. There were four separate splits in the continuum—creating a Ewing who died in Firnik's torture chamber, a Ewing who rescued the tortured Ewing and left a note and committed suicide, a Ewing who rescued the tortured Ewing and did *not* commit suicide, and a Ewing who was rescued and did not himself go back to become the rescuer, thereby breaking the chain. Two of these are still alive—the third and the fourth. You and me.''

Very quietly Ewing said, "I guess that makes sense, in an impossible sort of way. But that leaves an extra Baird Ewing, doesn't it? After you carried out the rescue, why did you decide to stay alive?''

The other shrugged. "I couldn't risk killing myself. I didn't know what would happen.''

"You did,'' Ewing said accusingly. "You knew that the next man in sequence would stay alive. You could have left him a note, but you didn't. So he went through the chain, left *me* a note, and removed himself.''

The other scowled unhappily, "Perhaps he represented a braver facet of us than I do.''

"How could that be? We're all the same?''

"True.'' The other smiled sadly. "But a human being is made of complex stuff. Life isn't a procession of clear-cut events; it's a progression from one tough decision to the next. The seeds of my decision were in the proto-Ewing; so were the bases for the suicide. I picked things one way; *he* picked them the other. And I'm here.''

Ewing realized it was impossible to be angry. The man he faced was himself, and he knew only too well the bundle of inner contradictions, of strengths and weaknesses, that was Baird Ewing—or any human being. This was no time to condemn. But he foresaw grave problems arising.

He said, "What do we do now—*both of us?*"

"There was a reason why I called you off the ship. And it wasn't simply that I didn't want to be left behind on Earth."

"What was it, then?"

"The time machine Myreck has can save Corwin from the Klodni," the other Ewing said flatly.

Ewing sat back and let that soak in. "How?"

"I went to see Myreck this morning and he greeted me with open arms. Said he was so glad I had come back for a look at the time machine. That was when I realized you'd been there yesterday and hadn't gone back on the merry-go-round." He shook his head. "I was counting on that, you see—on being the only Ewing that actually went forward on the time-track, while all the others went round and round between Fourday and Twoday, chasing themselves. But you broke the sequence and fouled things up."

"*You* fouled things up," Ewing snapped. "You aren't supposed to be alive."

"And you aren't supposed to be existing in Fiveday."

"This isn't helping things," Ewing said more calmly. "You say the Earther time machine can save Corwin. How?"

"I was getting to that. This morning Myreck showed me all the applications of the machine. It can be converted into an exterior-operating scanner—a beam that can be used to hurl objects of any size backward into time.''

"The Klodni fleet," Ewing said instantly.

"Exactly! we set up the projector on Corwin and wait for the Klodni to arrive—and shoot them back five billion years or so, with no return-trip ticket!''

Ewing smiled. "And I was running away. I was on my way home, while you were finding all this out.''

The other shrugged. "You had no reason to suspect it. You never had a first-hand demonstration of the way the time machine functioned. I did—and I guessed this might be possible. You guessed so, too.''

"Me?''

"Right after Myreck told you he had temporal control, the thought came to you that something like this might be worked out. But you forgot about it. I didn't.''

It was eerie, Ewing thought, to sit across a table from a man who knew every thought of his, every secret deed, from childhood up to a point three days ago in Absolute Time. After that, of course, their lives diverged as if they were different people.

"What do you suggest we do now?'' Ewing asked.

"Go back to Myreck. Team up to get the plans for the device away from him. Then high-tail it back here, get aboard . . .''

His voice trailed off. Ewing stared blankly at his alter ego and said, "Yes? What then? I'm waiting.''

"It's—it's a one-man ship isn't it?'' the other asked in a thin voice.

"Yes," Ewing said. "Damned right it is. After

we've taken the plans, how do we decide who goes back to Corwin and who stays here?''

He knew the other's anguished frown was mirrored by his own. He felt sick, and knew the other sensed the same unease. He felt the frustration of a man staring into a mirror, trying desperately to make some maneuver that would not be imitated by the imprisoned image.

''We'll worry about that later,'' said the other Ewing uncertainly. ''First let's get the plans from Myreck. Time to settle other problems later.''

They took a robot-operated cab to the surburban district where the College of Abstract Science was located. On the way, Ewing turned to the other and said, ''How did you know I was on my way home?''

''I didn't. As soon as I found out from Myreck both that you existed and that his machine could help Corwin, I got back to the Grand Valloin. I went straight up to your room, but the identity plate didn't work—and that door was geared to my identity just as much as yours. So I went downstairs, phoned the desk from the lobby, and asked for you. They told me you had checked out and were on your way to the spaceport. So I followed—and got there just in time.''

''And suppose I had refused to come out of the ship and meet you?'' Ewing asked.

''There would have been a mess. I would have insisted *I* was Ewing and you were stealing my ship—which would be true, in a way—and would have demanded they check me against their records of Ewing. They would have found out I was Ewing, of course, and they would have wondered who the deuce *you* were. There would have been an investigation, and you would have been grounded. But either way it would have been risky—either if they had discovered there actually was an extra Ewing, or if you had ignored the grounding orders and blasted off. They'd have sent an interceptor after you and we'd really be in trouble.''

The cab pulled up near the empty lot that was the College of Abstract Science. Ewing let his alternate pay the bill. They got out.

''You wait here,'' the other said. ''I'll put myself within their receptor field and wait for them to let me in. You wait ten minutes and follow me through.''

''I don't have a watch,'' Ewing said. ''Firnik took it.''

''Here—take mine,'' said the other impatiently. He unstrapped it and handed it over. It looked costly.

''Where'd you get this?'' Ewing said.

''I borrowed it from some Earther, along with about five hundred credits, early Threeday morning. You—no, not you, but the Ewing who became your rescuer later—was asleep in our hotel room, so I had to find another place to stay. And all I had was about ten credits left over after buying the mask and the gun.''

The ten credits someone left for me, Ewing thought. The paradoxes multiplied. The best he could do was ignore them.

He donned the watch—the time was 1850, Fivenight—and watched his companion stroll down the street toward the empty lot, wander with seeming aimlessness over the vacant area, and suddenly vanish. The College of Abstract Sciences had swallowed him up.

Ewing waited for the minutes to pass. They crept by. Five . . . six . . . seven.

At eight, he began to stroll with what he hoped looked like complete casualness toward the empty lot. At nine he was only a few yards away from the borders of the lot. He forced himself to remain quite still, letting the final minute pass. The stun-gun was at his hip. He had noticed that the other Ewing also wore a stun-gun—the twin of his own.

At nine minutes and forty-five seconds he resumed his stroll toward the lot, reaching it exactly at the ten-minute mark. He looked around the way the other Ewing had—and felt the transition from *now-minus-three-microseconds* sweep over him once again. He was inside the College of Abstract Science, having vanished abruptly from the tardy world outside.

He was facing an odd tableau. The other Ewing stood with his back to one wall, the stun-gun drawn and in activated position. Facing him were seven or eight members of the College, their faces pale, their eyes reflecting fright. They stood as if at bay.

Ewing found himself looking down at the acusing eyes of Scholar Myreck, who had admitted him.

"Thank you for letting my—ah—brother in," the other Ewing said. For a moment the two Ewings stared at each other. Ewing saw in his alter ego's eyes deep guilt, and knew that the other man was more than a twin to him than any brother could have been. The kinship was soul-deep.

"We're sorry for this," he said to Myreck. "Believe us, it pains us to do this to you."

"I've already explained what we came for," the other Ewing said. "There's a scale model and a full set of schematics downstairs, plus a few notebooks of theoretical work. It's more than one man can carry."

"The notebooks are irreplaceable," Myreck said in a softly bitter voice.

"We'll take good care of them," Ewing promised. "But we need them more than you. Believe us."

The other Ewing said, "You stay here, and keep your gun on them. I'm going below with Myreck to fetch the things we're taking."

Ewing nodded. Drawing his gun, he replaced the other against the wall, holding the unfortunate Earthers at bay. It was nearly five minutes before Ewing's alternate and Myreck returned, bearing papers, notebooks, and a model that looked to weigh about fifty pounds.

"It's all here," the other said. "Myreck, you're going to let me through your time-phase field and out of the building. My brother here will keep his gun on you all the time. Please don't try to trick us."

Ten minutes later, both Ewings stood outside the College of Abstract Science, with a nearly man-high stack of plunder between them.

"I hated to do that," Ewing said.

The other nodded. "It hurt me, too. They're so gentle—and it's a miserable way to repay hospitality. But we need that generator, if we want to save everything we hold dear."

"Yes," Ewing said in a strained voice. "Everything *we* hold dear." He shook his head. Trouble was approaching. "Come on," he said, looking back at the vacant lot. "Let's get out of here. We have to load all this stuff on the ship."

FIFTEEN

THEY MADE the trip back to the spaceport in tight silence. Each man had kept a hand atop the teetering stack on the floor of the cab; occasionally, Ewing's eyes met those of his double, and glanced guiltily away.

Which one of us goes back? he wondered.

Which one is really Baird Ewing? And what becomes of the other?

At the spaceport, Ewing requisitioned a porter-robot and turned the stolen schematics, notes, and model over to it, to be placed aboard the ship. That done, the two men looked strangely at each other. The time had come for departure. Who left?

Ewing scratched his chin uneasily and said, "One of us has to go up to the departure desk and reconfirm his blastoff plans. The other—"

"Yes. I know."

"How do we decide? Do we flip a coin?" Ewing wanted to know.

"One of us goes back to Laira and Blade. And it looks as if the other—"

There was no need to say it. The dilemma was insoluble. Each Ewing had firmly believed he was the only one still in the time-track, and each still partially believed that it was the other's duty to yield.

The spaceport lights flickered dizzily. Ewing felt dryness grow in his throat. The time for decision was now. But how to decide?

"Let's go get a drink," he suggested.

The entrance to the refreshment booth was congested with a mob of evening travelers hoping to get a last drink down before blasting off. Ewing ordered drinks for both of them and they toasted grimly: "To Baird Ewing—whichever he may be."

Ewing drank, but the drink did not soothe him. It seemed at that moment that the impasse might last forever, that they would remain on Earth eternally while determining which one of them was to return with Corwin's salvation and which to remain behind. But an instant later, all that was changed.

The public address system blared: *"Attention, please! Your attention! Will everyone kindly remain precisely where he is right at this moment!"*

Ewing exchanged a troubled glance with his counterpart. The loud-speaker voice continued, *"There is no cause for alarm. It is believed that a dangerous criminal is at large somewhere in the spaceport area. He may be armed. He is six feet two inches in height, with reddish-brown hair, dark eyes, and out-of-fashion clothing. Please remain precisely where you are at this moment while peace officers circulate among you. Have your identification papers ready to*

128

be examined on request. That is all."

A burst of conversation greeted the announcement. The two Ewings huddled each into the corner of the room and stared in anguish at each other.

"Someone turned us in," Ewing said. "Myreck, perhaps. Or the man you burgled. Probably Myreck."

"It doesn't matter who turned us in," the other snapped. "All that matters is the fact that they'll be coming around to investigate soon. And when they find *two* men answering to the description—"

"Myreck must have warned them there were two of us."

"No. He'd never do that. He doesn't want to give away the method that brought both of us into existence, does he?"

Ewing nodded. "I guess you're right. But if they find two of us with the same identity papers—with the same identity—they'll pull us both in. And neither of us will ever get back to Corwin."

"Suppose they only found one of us?" the other asked.

"How? We can't circulate around the spaceport. And there's no place to hide in here."

"I don't mean that. Suppose one of us voluntarily gave himself up—destroyed his identity papers first, of course, and then made an attempt to escape? In the confusion, the other of us could safely blast off for Corwin."

Ewing's eyes narrowed. He had been formulating just such a plan, too. "But which one of us gives himself up? We're back to the same old problem."

"No, we're not," the other said. "I'll volunteer!

"No," Ewing said instantly. "You can't just volunteer! How could I agree? It's suicide." He shook his head. "We don't have time to argue about it now. There's only one way to decide."

He fumbled in his pocket and pulled forth a shining half-credit piece. He studied it. On one side was engraved a representation of Earth's sun, with the nine planets orbiting it; on the other, an ornamental *50*.

"I'm going to flip it," he said. "Solar system, you go; denomination, I go. Agreed?"

"Agreed," said the other tensely.

Ewing mounted the coin on his thumbnail and flicked it upward. He snapped it out of the air with a rapid gesture and slapped it down against the back of his left hand. He lifted the covering hand.

It was denomination. The stylized *50* stared up at him.

He smiled humorlessly. "I guess it's me," he said. He pulled his identity papers from his pocket and ripped them into shreds. Then he stared across the table at the white, drawn face of the man who was to become Baird Ewing. "So long. Good luck. And kiss Laira for me when you get back. . . ."

Four Sirian policemen entered the bar and began to filter through the group. One remained stationed near the door; the other three circulated. Ewing rose from his seat; he felt calm now. It was not as if he were really going to die. *Which is the real me, anyway? The man who died in the torture chamber, or the one who blew himself up in the energitron booth, or the man sitting back there in the corner of the bar? They're all Baird Ewing. There's a continuity of personality. Baird Ewing won't die—just one of his superfluous Doppelgängers. And it has to be this way.*

Icily, Ewing made his way through the startled group sitting at the tables. He was the only figure moving in the bar except for the three circulating police officers. who did not appear to have noticed him yet. He did not look back.

The stun-gun at his hip was only inches from his hand. He jerked it up suddenly and fired at the policeman mounted by the door; the man froze and toppled. The other three policemen whirled.

Ewing heard one of them, "Who are you? What are you doing there? Stand still!"

"I'm the man you're looking for," Ewing shouted, in a voice that could have been heard for hundreds of yards. "If you want me, come get me!"

He turned and sprinted out of the refreshment room into the long arcade.

He heard the sound of pursuers almost immediately. He clutched the stun-gun tightly, but did not fire. An energy flare spashed above his head, crumbling a section of the wall. He heard a yell from behind him: "Stop him! There's the man! Stop him!"

As if summoned magically, five policemen appeared at the upper end of the corridor. Ewing thumbed his stunner and froze two of them; then he cut briskly to the left, passing through an automatic door and entering onto the restricted area of the spacefield itself.

A robot came gliding up to him. "May I see your pass, sir? Humans are not allowed on this portion of the field without a pass."

In answer, Ewing tilted the stun-gun up and calcified the robot's neural channels. It crashed heavily as its gyrocontrol destablized. He turned. The police were converging on him; there were dozens of them.

"You there! Give yourself up! You can't hope to escape!"

I know that, Ewing said silently. *But I don't want to be taken alive, either.*

He wedged himself flat against a parked fueler and peppered the advancing police with stun-gun beams. They fired cautiously; there was expensive equipment on the field, and they preferred to take their man alive in any event. Ewing waited until the nearest of them was within fifty yards.

"Come get me," he called. Turning, he began to run across the broad spacefield.

The landing apron extended for two or three miles; he ran easily, lightly, sweeping in broad circles and pausing to fire at his pursuers. He wanted to keep them at reasonable distance until—

Yes. Now.

Darkness covered the field. Ewing glanced up to see the cause of this sudden eclipse.

A vast ship hung high overhead, descending as if operated by a pulley and string. Its jets were thundering, pouring forth flaming gas as it came down for a landing. Ewing smiled at the sight.

It'll be quick, he thought.

He heard the yells of astonishment from the police. They were backing off as the great ship dropped toward the landing area. Ewing ran in a wider circle, trying to compute the orbit of the descending liner.

Like falling into the sun. Hot. Quick.

He saw the place where the ship would land. He felt the sudden warmth; he was in the danger zone now. He ran inward, where the air was frying. *For Corwin,* he thought. *For Laira. And Blade.*

"The idiot! He'll get killed!" someone screamed as if from a great distance. Eddies of flaming gas seemed to wash down over him; he heard the booming roar of the ship. Then brightness exploded all about him, and consciousness and pain departed in a microsecond.

The ship touched down.

In the terminal, the public address system blared: "*Attention, please. We thank you very much for your coöperation. The criminal has been discovered and is no longer menacing society. You may resume normal activity. We thank you again for your coöperation during this investigation, and hope you have undergone no inconvenience.*"

In the terminal refreshment room, Ewing stared bleakly at the two half-finished drinks on the table—his, and the dead man's. With a sudden, brusque gesture he poured the other drink into his glass, stirred the two together, and drank the glassful down in eager gulps. He felt the stinging liquor jolt into his stomach.

What are you supposed to say and think and do, he wondered, *when a man gives up his life so you can get away? Nothing. You can't even say "Thanks." It wouldn't be in good taste, would it?*

He had watched the whole thing from the observation window of the bar. The desperate pursuit, the fox-and-hounds chase, the exchange of shots. He had become sickly aware that a liner was overhead, fixed in its landing orbit, unable to check its fall whether there was one man or a regiment drilling on the field.

Even though the window's protective glass, the sudden glare had stung his retinas. And throughout his life he would carry with him the image of a tiny man-shaped dot standing unafraid in the bright path of the liner, vanishing suddenly in a torrent of flame.

He rose. He felt very tired, very weary, not at all like a man free at last to return to his home, his wife, his child. His mission was approaching to a successful conclusion, but he felt no sense of satisfaction. Too many had given up life or dreams to make his success possible.

He found the departure desk somehow, and pulled forth the papers that the dead man who was himself had filled out earlier in the day. "My ship's on Blasting Area Eleven," he told the robot. "I was originally scheduled to leave about 1700 this evening, but I requested cancellation and rescheduling."

He waited numbly while the robot went through the proper proceedures, gave him new papers to fill out, and finally sent him on through the areaway to the departure track. Another robot met him there and conducted him to the ship.

His ship. Which might have left for Corwin five hours before, with a different pilot.

Ewing shrugged and tried to brush away the cloud of gloom. Had the ship left earlier, with the other Ewing aboard, it would have been to conclude an unsuccessful mission; the delay of five hours made an infinite difference in the general effect.

And it was foolishness to talk of a man dead. Who had died? Baird Ewing? I'm still alive, he thought. So who died?

He entered the ship and glanced around. Everything was ready for departure. He frowned; the other Ewing had said something about having sent a message back to Corwin presumably telling them he was on his way back empty-handed. He activated the subetheric communicator and beamed a new message, advising them to disregard the one immediately preceding it, saying that a new development had come up and he was on his way back to Corwin with possible salvation.

He called the central control tower and requested blast-off permission twelve minutes hence. That gave him ample time. He switched on the autopilot, stripped, and lowered himself into the nutrient bath.

With quick foot-motions he set in motion the suspension mechanism. Needles jabbed at his flesh; the temperature began its downward climb. A thin stream of web came from the spinnerettes above him, wrapping him in unbreakable foam that would protect him from the hazards of high-acceleration blast-off.

The drugs dulled his mind. He felt a faint chill as the temperature about him dropped below sixty. It would drop much lower than that, later, when he was asleep. He waited drowsily for sleep to overtake him.

He was only fractionally conscious when blast-off came. He barely realized that the ship had left Earth. Before acceleration ended, he was totally asleep.

SIXTEEN

HOURS TICKED BY, and Ewing slept. Hours lengthened into days, into weeks, into months. Eleven months, twelve days, seven and one half hours, and Ewing slept while the tiny ship speared along on its return journey.

The time came. The ship pirouetted out of warp when the pre-set detectors indicated the journey had ended. Automatic computer units hurled the ship into fixed orbit round the planet below. The suspension unit deactivated itself; temperature gradually returned to normal, and a needle plunged into Ewing's side, awakening him.

He was home.

After the immediate effects of the long sleep had worn off, Ewing made contact with the authorities below. He waited, hunched over the in-system communicator, staring through the vision-plate at the blue loveliness of his home planet.

After a moment, a response came:

"World Building, Corwin. We have your call. Please identify."

Ewing replied with the series of code symbols that had been selected as identification. He repeated them three times, reeling them off from memory.

The acknowledging symbols came back instantly, after which the same voice said, "Ewing? At last!"

"It's only been a couple of years, hasn't it?" Ewing said. "Nothing's changed too much."

"No. Not too much."

There was a curious, strained tone in the voice that made Ewing feel uneasy, but he did not prolong the conversation. He jotted down the landing coördinates as they came in, integrated and fed them to his computer, and proceeded to carry out the landing.

He came down at Broughton Spacefield, fifteen miles outside Corwin's capital city, Broughton. The air was bright and fresh, with the extra tang that he had missed during his stay on Earth. After descending from his ship he waited for the pickup truck. He stared at the blue arch of the sky, dotted with clouds, and at the magnificent row of 800-foot-high Imperator trees that bordered the spacefield. Earth had no trees to compare with those, he thought.

The truck picked him up; a grinning field hand said, "Welcome back, Mr. Ewing!"

"Thanks," Ewing said, climbing aboard. "It's good to be back."

A hastily-assembled delegation was on hand at the terminal building when the truck arrived. Ewing recognized Premier Davidson, three or four members of the Council, a few people from the University. He looked around, wondering just why it was that Laira and his son had not come to welcome him home.

Then he saw them, standing with some of his friends in the back of the group. They came forward, Laira with an odd little smile on her face, young Blade with a blank stare for a man he had probably almost forgotten.

"Hello, Baird," Laira said. Her voice was higher than he had remembered it as being, and she looked older than the mental image he carried. Her eyes had deepened, her face grown thin. "It's so good to have you back. Blade, say hello to your father."

Ewing looked at the boy. He had grown tall and gangling; the chubby eight-year-old he had left behind had turned into a coltish boy of nearly eleven. He eyed his father uncertainly. "Hello—Dad."

"Hello there, Blade!"

He scooped the boy off the ground, tossed him easily into the air, caught him, set him down. He turned to Laira, then, and kissed her. But there was no warmth in his greeting. A strange thought interposed:

Am I really Baird Ewing?

Am I the man who was born on Corwin, married this woman, built my home, fathered this child? Or did he die back on Earth, and am I just a replica indistinguishable from the original?

It was a soul-numbing thought. He realized it was foolish of him to worry over the point; he wore Baird Ewing's body, he carried Baird Ewing's memory and personality. What else was there to a man, besides his physical existence and the tenuous Gestalt of memories and thoughts that might be called his soul?

I am Baird Ewing, he insisted inwardly, trying to

quell the doubt rising within him.

They were all looking earnestly at him. He hoped none of his inner distress was visible. Turning to Premier Davidson, he said, "Did you get my messages?"

"All three of them—there *were* only three, weren't there?"

"Yes," Ewing said. "I'm sorry about those last two—"

"It really stirred us up, when we got that message saying you were coming home without anything gained. We were really counting on you, Baird. And then, about four hours later, came the second message—"

Ewing chuckled with a warmth he did not feel. "Something came up at the very last minute. Something that can save us from the Klodni." He glanced around uncertainly. "What's the news there? How about the Klodni?"

"They've conquered Borgman," Davidson said. "We're next. Within a year, they say. They changed their direction after Lundquist—"

"They got Lundquist too?" Ewing interrupted.

"Lundquist and Borgman both. Six planets, now. And we're next on the list."

Ewing shook his head slowly. "No, we're not. They're on *our* list. I've brought something back from Earth with me, and the Klodni won't like it."

He went before the Council that evening, after having been allowed to spend the afternoon at home, renewing his acquaintance with his family, repairing the breach two years of absence had created.

He took with him the plans and drawings and model he had wrung from Myreck and the College. He explained precisely how he planned to defeat the Klodni. The storm burst the moment he had finished.

Jospers, the delegate from Northwest Corwin, immediately broke out with; "Time travel? Impossible!"

Four of the other delegates echoed the thought. Premier Davidson pounded for order. Ewing shouted them down and said, "Gentlemen, I'm not asking you to believe what I tell you. You sent me to Earth to bring back help, and I've brought it."

"But it's fantastic to tell us—"

"Please, Mr. Jospers. This thing *works*."

"How do you know?"

Ewing took a deep breath. He had not wanted to reveal this. "I've tried it," he said. "I've gone back in time. I've talked face-to-face with myself. You don't have to believe that, either. You can squat here like a bunch of sitting ducks and let the Klodni blast us the way they've blasted Barnholt and Borgman and Lundquist, and all the other colony worlds in this segment of space. But I tell you I have a workable defense here."

Quietly Davidson said, "Tell us this, Baird: how much will it cost us to build this—ah—weapon of yours, and how long will it take?"

Ewing considered the questions a moment. He said, "I would estimate at least six to eight months of full-time work by a skilled group of engineers to make the thing work in the scale I intend. As for the cost, I don't see how it could be done for less than three million stellors."

Jospers was on his feet in an instant. "Three million stellors! I ask you, gentlemen—"

His question never was asked. In a voice that tolerated no interruptions, Ewing said, "I ask *you,* gentlemen—how much is life worth to you, and expensive nonsense as well. But what of the cost? In a year the Klodni will be here, and your economies won't matter a damn. Unless you plan to beat them your own way, of course."

"Three million stellors represents twenty percent of our annual budget," Davidson remarked. "Should your device prove to be of no help—"

"Don't you see?" Ewing shouted. "It doesn't *matter!* If my device doesn't work, there won't be any more budgets for you to worry about!"

It was an unanswerable point. Grudgingly, Jospers conceded, and with his concession the opposition collapsed. It was agreed that the weapon brought back from Earth by Ewing would be built. There was no choice. The shadow of the advancing Klodni grew longer and longer on the stars, and no other weapon existed. Nothing known to man could stop the advancing hordes.

Possibly, something unknown could.

Ewing had been a man who enjoyed privacy, but now there was no privacy for him. His home became a perpetual open house; the ministers of state were forever conferring with him, discussing the new project. People from the University wanted to know about Earth. Publishers prodded Ewing to write books for them; magazines and telestat firms begged for copy.

He refused them all. He was not interested in capitalizing on his trip to Earth.

He spent most of his time at the laboratory that had been given him in North Broughton, supervising the development of the time projector. He had no formal scientific training himself; the actual work was under the control of a staff of engineers from the University. But he aided them with suggestions and theoretical contributions, based on his conversations with Myreck and his own experiences with the phenomenon of time transfer.

The weeks passed. At home, Ewing found family life strained and tense. Laira was almost a stranger to him; he told her what he could of his brief stay on Earth, but he had earlier determined to keep the account of his time-shift to himself forever, and his story was sketchy and inconsistent.

As for Blade, he grew used to his father again. But Ewing did not feel comfortable with either of them. They were, perhaps, not really his; and, preposterous though the thought was, he could not fully accept the reality of his existence.

There had been other Ewings. He was firmly convinced he had been the first of the four, that the others had merely been duplicates of him, but there was no certainty in that. And two of those duplicates had given up their lives so that he might be home on Corwin.

He brooded over that, and also about Myreck and about Earth. Earth, which by now was merely a Sirian protectorate. Earth, which had sent her boldest sons forth to the stars, and had withered her own substance at hime.

He saw pictures of the devastation on Lundquist

and Borgman. Lundquist had been a pleasure world, attracting visitors from a dozen worlds to its games parlors and lovely gardens, luminous and radiant. The pictures showed the lacy towers of Lundquist's dreamlike cities crumbling under the merciless Klodni guns. Senselessly, brutally, the Klodni were moving forward.

Scouts checked their approach. The fleet was massed on Borgman, now. If they held to their regular pattern, it would be nearly a year before they rumbled out of the Borgman system to make their attack on nearby Cowin. And a year would be enough time.

Ewing counted the passing days. The conical structure of the time-projector took shape slowly, as the technicians, working from Myreck's model, carried out their painstaking tasks. No one asked exactly how the weapon would be put in use. Ewing had specified that it be installed in a space ship, and it had been designed accordingly.

At night he was haunted by the recurring image of the Ewing who had willingly thrown himself under the jets of a descending spaceliner. *It could have been me,* he thought. *I volunteered. But he wanted to toss for it.*

And there had been another Ewing, equally brave, whom he had never known. The man who had taken the steps that would render him superfluous, and then had calmly and simply removed himself from existence.

I didn't do that. I figured the others would be caught in the wheel forever, and that I'd be the only one who would get loose. But it didn't happen that way.

He was haunted too, by the accusing stare in

Myreck's eyes as the twin Corwinites plundered the College of its secrets and abandoned Earth to its fate. Here, again, Ewing had his rationalizations: there was nothing he could have done to help. Earth was the prisoner of its own woes.

Laira told him finally that he had changed, that he had become bitter, almost irasible, since making the journey to Earth.

"I don't understand it, Baird. You used to be so warm, so—so *human*. And you're different now. Cold, turned inward, brooding all the time." She touched his arm lightly. "Can't you talk things out with me? Something's troubling you. Something that happened on Earth, maybe?"

He whirled away. "*No!* Nothing." He realized his tone was harsh; he saw the pain on her face. In a softer voice he said, "I can't help myself, Laira. There's nothing I can say. I've been under a strain, that's all."

The strain of seeing myself die, and of seeing a culture die. Of journeying through time and across space. I've been through a lot. Too much, maybe.

He felt very tired. He looked up at the night sky as it glittered over the viewing-porch of their home. The stars were gems mounted on black velvet. There were the familiar constellations, the Turtle and the Dove, the Great Wheel, the Spear. He had missed those configurations of stars while he was on Earth. They had seemed to him friendly aspects of home.

But there was nothing friendly about the cold stars tonight. Ewing held his wife close and stared up at them, and it seemed to him that they held a savage menace. As if the Klodni hordes hovered there like moisture particles in a rain cloud, waiting for their moment to descend.

SEVENTEEN

THE ALARM came early on a spring morning, a year after Ewing had returned to Corwin. It was a warm, muggy morning. A soft rain was falling, automatically energizing the deflectors on the roof of Ewing's home; their polarizing cells kept the rain from tattooing on the flat roof. Ewing lay in uneasy sleep.

The phone rang. He stirred, turned over, buried his face in the pillow. He was dreaming of a figure limned briefly in a white flare of jet exhaust on Valloin Spacefield. The phone continued to ring.

Groggily, Ewing felt a hand shaking him. A voice—Laira's voice—was saying, ''Wake up, Baird! There's a call for you! Wake up!''

Reluctantly, he came awake. The wall clock said 0430. He rubbed his eyes, crawled out of the bed, groped his way across the room to the phone extension. He choked back a yawn.

''Ewing here. What is it?''

The sharp, high pitched tones of Premier Davidson

cut into his sleep-drugged mind. "Baird, the Klodni are on their way!"

He was fully awake now. "What?"

"We just got word from the scout network," Davidson said. "The main Klodni attacking fleet left Borgman about four hours ago, and there are at least five hundred ships in the first wave."

"When are they expected to reach this area?"

"We have conflicting estimates on that. It isn't easy to compute super-light velocities. But on the basis of what we know, I'd say they'll be within firing range of Corwin in not less than ten nor more than eighteen hours, Baird."

Ewing nodded. "All right. Have the special ship serviced for immediate blast-off. I'll drive right out to the spaceport and pick it up there."

"Baird—"

"What is it?" Ewing asked impatiently.

"Don't you think—well, that some younger man should handle this job? I don't mean that you're *old*, but you have a wife, a son—and it's risky. One man against five hundred ships? It's suicide, Baird."

The word triggered dormant associations in Ewing, and he winced. Doggedly he said, "The Council has approved what I'm doing. This is no time to train someone else. We've been over this ground before."

He dressed rapidly, wearing, for sentiment's sake, the blue-and-gold uniform of the Corwin Space Force, in which he had served the mandatory two-year term a dozen years before. The uniform was tight, but still fitted.

While Laira fixed a meal he stood by a window, looking outward at the gray, swirling, pre-dawn mists. He had lived so long in the shadow of the Klodni advance that he found it hard to believe the day had actually come.

He ate moodily, scarcely tasting the food as he swallowed it, saying nothing.

Laira said, "I'm frightened, Baird."

"Frightened?" He chuckled. "Of what?"

She did not seem amused. "Of the Klodni. Of this crazy thing you're going to do." After a moment she added, "But you don't seem afraid, Baird. And I guess that's all that matters."

"I'm not," he said truthfully. "There's nothing to be afraid of. The Klodni won't even be able to see me. There isn't a mass-detector in the universe sensitive enough to spot a one-man ship a couple of light-years away. The mass is insignificant; and there'll be too much background noise coming out of the fleet itself."

Besides, he added silently, *how can I be afraid of these Klodni?*

They were not even human. They were faceless, mindless brutes, a murdering ant-horde marching through the worlds out of some fierce inner compulsion to slay. They were dangerous, but not frightening.

Fright had to be reserved for the real ememies— the human beings who turned against other humans, who played a double game of trust and betrayal. There was cause to respect the strength of the Klodni, but not to dread them for it. Dread was more appropriate applied to Rollun Firnik and his kind, Ewing thought.

When he had eaten, he stopped off briefly in Blade's bedroom to take a last look at the sleeping boy. He did not wake him. He merely looked in, smiled, and closed the door.

"Maybe you should wake him up and say goodbye," Laira suggested hesitantly.

Ewing shook his head. "It's too early. He needs his sleep at his age. Anyway, when I get back I guess I'll be a hero. He'll like that."

He caught the expression on her face, and added, "I *am* coming back. You could gamble our savings on it."

Dawn streaked the sky by the time he reached Broughton Spacefield. He left his car with an attendant and went to the main administration building, where a grim-faced group of Corwin officials waited for him.

This is it, Ewing thought. *If I don't make it, Corwin's finished.*

A world's destiny rode on the wild scheme of one man. It was a burden he did not relish carrying.

He greeted Davidson and the others a little stiffly; the tension was beginning to grip him now. Davidson handed him a portfolio.

"This is the flight chart of the Klodni armada," the Premier explained. "We had the big computer extrapolate it. They'll be overhead in nine hours and fifty minutes."

Ewing shook his head. "You're wrong. They won't be overhead at all. I'm going to meet them at least a light-year from here, maybe further out if I can manage it. They won't get any closer."

He scanned the charts. Graphs of the Klodni force had been inked in.

"The computer says there are seven hundred

seventy-five ships in the fleet,'' Davidson said.

Ewing pointed to the formation. ''It's a pure wedge, isn't it? A single flagship, followed by two ships, followed by a file of four, followed by eight. And right on out to here. That's very interesting.''

''It's a standard Klodni fighting formation,'' said gravel-voiced Dr. Harmess of the Department of Military Science. ''The flagship always leads and none of the others dares to break formation without order. Complete totalitarian discipline.''

Ewing smiled. ''I'm glad to hear it.''

He checked his watch. Approximately ten hours from now, Klodni guns would be thundering down on a virtually defenseless Corwin. A fleet of seven hundred seventy-five dreadnoughts was an unstoppable armada. Corwin had perhaps a dozen ships, and not all of them in fighting trim despite vigorous last-minute work. No planet in the civilized galaxy could stand the burden of supporting a military force of nearly eight hundred first-line ships.

''All right,'' he said after a moment's silence. ''I'm ready to leave.''

They led him across the damp, rain-soaked field to the well-guarded special hangar where Project X had been installed. Security guards smiled obligingly and stood to one side when they recognized Ewing and the Premier. Field attendants swung open the doors of the hangar, revealing the ship.

It was a thin black spear, hardly bigger than the vessel that had taken him to Earth and back. Inside, though, there was no complex equipment for suspending animation. In its place, there now rested a tubular helical coil, whose tip projected micromillimeters from the skin of the ship. At the base of the coil was a complex control panel.

Ewing nodded in approval. The field attendants wheeled the ship out; gantry cranes tilted it to blasting angle and carried it to the blast-field.

A black ship against the blackness of space. The Klodni would never notice it, Ewing thought. He sensed the joy of battle springing up in him.

"I'll leave immediately," he said.

The actual blast-off was to be handled automatically. Ewing clambored aboard, settled himself in the cradle area, and let the spinnerettes weave him an unshatterable cradle of spidery foamweb. He switched on the vision-plate and saw the little group waiting tensely at the edge of the clear part of the field.

He did not envy them. Of necessity, he would have to maintain total radio silence until after the encounter. For half a day or more, they would wait, not knowing whether death would come to their world or not. It would be an uncomfortable day for them.

With an almost impulsive gesture Ewing tripped the blasting lever, and lay back as the ship raced upward. For the second time in his life he was leaving Corwin's soil.

The ship arced upward in a wide hyperbolic orbit, while Ewing shuddered in his cradle and waited. Seconds later, the jets cut out. The rest of the journey would be carried out on warp-drive. That was less strenuous, at least.

The pre-plotted course carried him far from Corwin during the first two hours. A quick triangulation showed that he was almost one and a half light-years from the home world—a safe enough distance, he thought. He ceased forward thrust and put the ship in a closed million-mile orbit perpendicular to the expected line of attack of the Klodni. He waited.

Three hours slipped by before the first quiver of green appeared on his ship's mass-detector. The line wavered uncertainly. Ewing resolved the fine focus and waited.

The line broadened. And broadened. And broadened again.

The Klodni wedge was drawing near.

Ewing felt utterly calm, now that the waiting was over. Moving smoothly and unhurriedly, he proceeded to activate the time-transfer equipment. He yanked down on the main lever, and the control panel came to life; the snout of the helical core advanced nearly an inch from the skin of the ship, enough to insure a clear trajectory.

Working with one eye on the mass-detector and one on the transfer device's control panel, Ewing computed the necessary strength of the field. The Klodni formation opened out geometrically: one ship leading, followed by two, with four in the third rank, eight in the fourth, sixteen in the fifth. Two massive ranks of about two hundred fifty ships each served as rearguard for the wedge, providing a double finishing-thrust for any attack. It was the width of these last two files that mattered most.

No doubt they were traveling in a three-dimensional array, but Ewing took no chances, and assumed that all two hundred and fifty were moving in a single parallel bar. He computed the maximum width of such a formation. He added twenty percent at each side. If only a dozen Klodni ships slipped through, Corwin still would face a siege of havoc.

Compiling his data, he fed it to the transfer machine and established the necessary coördinates. He punched out the activator signals. He studied the mass-detector; the Klodni fleet was less than an hour away, now.

He nodded in satisfaction as the last of his computations checked and canceled out. Here goes, he thought.

He tripped the actuator.

There was no apparent effect, no response except for a phase-shift on one of the meters aboard the ship. But Ewing knew there had been an effect. A gulf had opened in the heavens, an invisible gulf that radiated outward from his ship and sprawled across space.

A gulf he could control as a fisherman might, a net—a net wide enough to hold seven hundred seventy-five alien vessels of war.

Ewing waited.

His tiny ship swung in its rigid orbit, round and round, carrying the deadly nothingness round with it. The Klodni fleet drew near. Ewing scratched out further computations. At no time, he thought, would he be closer to a Klodni ship than forty-light minutes. They would never pick him up at such a distance.

A minnow huddled in the dark, waiting to trap the whales.

The green line on the mass-detector broadened and became intense. Ewing shifted out of his locked orbit, placing the vessel on manual response. He readied his trap as the Klodni flagship moved serenely on through the void.

Now! he thought.

He cast his net.

The Klodni flagship moved on—and vanished! From Ewing's vantage point it seemed as if the great vessel had simply been blotted out; the green wedge on the scope of his mass-detector was blunt-snouted now that the flagship was gone.

But to the ships behind it, nothing seemed amiss. Without breaking formation they followed on, and Ewing waited. The second rank vanished through the gulf, and the third, and the fourth.

Eighteen ships gone. Thirty-two. Sixty-four.

He held his breath as the hundred-twenty-eight-ship rank entered the *cul-de-sac*. Now for the test. He stared at the mass-detector intently as the two biggest Klodni formations moved toward him. Two hundred fifty ships each, the hammers of the Klodni forces—

Gone.

The mass-detector was utterly blank. There was not a Klodni ship anywhere within detectable range. Ewing felt limp with relief. He disconnected the transfer mechanism, clamping down knife-switches with frenzied zeal. The gulf was sealed, now. There was no possible way back for the trapped Klodni ships.

He could break radio silence now. He sent a brief, laconic message: "Klodni fleet destroyed. Am returning to home base."

One man had wiped out an armada. He chuckled in relief of the crushing tension.

He wondered briefly how the puzzled Klodni would react when they found themselves in the midst of a trackless void, without stars, without planets. No doubt they would proceed on across space in search of some place to land, until their provisions became exhausted, their fuel disappeared, and death finally claimed them. Eventually, even their ships would crumble and disappear.

According to the best scientific theory, the stars of the galaxy were between five and six billion years old. the range of the Earther time-projector was nearly infinite.

Ewing had hurled the Klodni fleet five billion years into the past. He shuddered at the thought, and turned his tiny ship homeward, to Corwin.

EIGHTEEN

THE RETURN voyage seemed to take days. Ewing lay
awake in the protecting cradle, staring through the
open vision-plate at the blurred splendor of the
heavens as the ship shot through notspace at super-
light velocities. At these speeds, the stars appeared
as blotchy pastel things; the constellations did not
exist.

Curiously, he felt no sense of triumph. He had
saved Corwin, true—and in that sense, he had
achieved the goal in whose name he had set out on his
journey across space to Earth. But he felt as if his
work were incomplete.

He thought, not of Corwin now, but of Earth. Two
years had gone by on the mother world since his
departure; certainly, time enough for the Sirians to
make their move. Firnik, no doubt, was high in
command of the Sirian Governor-General instead of
holding a mere vice-consul's job. Byra Clork was
probably a noblewoman of the new aristocracy.

And Myreck and the others—well, perhaps they had survived, hidden three microseconds out of phase. But more likely they had been caught and put to death, like the potential dangers they were.

Dangers. There were no true dangers to the Sirians. Earth was self-weakened; it had no capacity to resist tyranny.

Guiltily, Ewing told himself that there was nothing he could have done. Earth's doom was foreordained, self-inflicted. He had saved his own world; there was no helping Earth.

There was a way, something in his mind said reproachfully. *There still is a way.*

Leave Corwin. Cross space once again, return to Earth, lead the hapless little Earthers in a struggle for freedom. All they needed was a man with the bold vigor of the outworld colonies. Leadership was what they lacked. They outnumbered the Sirians a thousand to one. In any kind of determined rising, they could win their freedom easily. But they needed a focal pocnt; they needed a leader.

You could be that leader, something within him insisted. *Go back to Earth.*

Savagely, he forced the idea to die. His place was on Corwin, where he was a hero, where his wife and child awaited him. Earth had to work out its own pitiful destiny.

He tried to relax. The ship plummeted onward through the night, toward Corwin.

It seemed that the whole populace turned out to welcome him. He could see them from above, as he maneuvered the ship through the last of its series of inward spirals and let it come gently to rest on the ferroconcrete landing surface of Broughton Spacefield.

He let the decontaminating squad do its work, while he watched the massed crowd assembled beyond the barriers. Finally, when the ship and the area around it were both safely cool, he stepped out.

The roar was deafening.

There were thousands of them. In the front he saw Laira and Blade, and the Premier, and the Council. University people. Newsmen. People, people, people. Ewing's first impulse was to shrink back into the lonely comfort of his ship. Instead, he compelled himself to walk forward toward the crowd. He wished they would stop shouting; he held up a hand, hoping to get silence, but the gesture was interpreted as a greeting and called forth an even noisier demonstration.

Somehow, he reached Laira and got his arms around her. He smiled; she said something, but her voice was crushed by the uproar. He read her lips instead. She was saying, "I was counting the seconds till you got back, darling."

He kissed her. He hugged Blade to him. He smiled to Davidson and to all of them, and wondered quietly why he had been born with the particular conglomeration of personality traits that had brought him to this destiny, on this world, on this day.

He was a hero. He had ended a threat that had destroyed six worlds.

Corwin was safe.

He was swept inside, carried off to the World Building, smuggled into Premier Davidson's private chambers. There, while officers of the peace kept the curiosity seekers away, Ewing dictated for the airwaves a full account of what he had done, while smiling friends looked on.

There were parades outside. He could hear the noise where he sat, seventy-one floors above the street level. It was hardly surprising; a world that had lived under sentence of death for five years found itself miraculously reprieved. It was small wonder the emotional top was blowing off.

Sometime toward evening, they let him go home. He had not slept for more than thirty hours, and it was beginning to show.

A cavalcade of official cars convoyed him out of the capital city and toward the surburban area where he lived. They told him a guard would be placed round his house, to assure him continued privacy. He thanked them all, and wished them good night, and entered his house. The door shut behind him, shutting out the noise, the celebration, the acclaim. He was just Baird Ewing of Corwin again, in his own home. He felt very tired. He felt hollow within, as if he were a villain rather than a hero. And it showed.

Laira said, "That trip didn't change you, did it?"

He blinked at her. "What do you mean?"

"I thought that the cloud would lift from you. That you were worried about the invasion and everything. But I guess I was wrong. We're safe, now—and something's still eating you."

He tried to laugh it off. "Laira, you're overtired. You've been worrying too much yourself. Why don't you get some sleep?"

She shook her head. "No, Baird. I'm serious. I

know you too well; I see something in your eyes. Trouble, of some kind.'' She put her hands round his wrists and stared up into his eyes. ''Baird, something happened to you on Earth that you haven't told me about. I'm your wife. I ought to know about it, if there's anything—''

''There's *nothing!* Nothing.'' He looked away. ''Let's go to sleep, Laira. I'm exhausted.''

But he lay in bed turning restlessly, and despite his exhaustion sleep did not come.

How can I go back to Earth? he asked himself bitterly. *My loyalties lie here. Earth will have to take care of itself—and if it can't, more's the pity.*

It was a hollow rationalization, and he knew it. He lay awake half the night, brooding, twisting, drowning in his own agonized perspiration.

He thought:

Three men died so I could return to Corwin safely. Two of them were deliberate, voluntary suicides. I owe them a debt. I owe Earth a debt, for making possible Corwin's salvation.

Three men died for me. Do I have any right to be selfish?

Then he thought:

When Laira married me, she thought she was getting Citizen Baird Ewing, period. She wasn't marrying any hero, any world saver. She didn't ask the Council to pick me for its trip to Earth. But she went through two years of widowhood because they did pick me.

How could I tell her I was leaving, going to Earth for good? Leaving her without a husband, and Blade without a father? It simply isn't fair to them. I can't do it.

And then he thought:

There must be a compromise. A way I can serve the memory of the dead Baird Ewings and be fair to my family as well. There has to be some kind of compromise.

There was. The answer came to him shortly before morning, crystal sharp, bearing with it no doubts, no further anxiety. He saw what his path must be. With the answer came a welling tide of peace, and he drifted into sound sleep, confident he had found the right way at last.

Premier Davidson, on behalf of the grateful people of the world of Corwin, called on him the next morning. Davidson told him he might pick anything, anything at all as his reward.

Ewing chuckled. "I've got everything I want already," he said. "Fame, fortune, family—what else is there in life?"

Shrugging, the rotund little Premier said, "But surely there must be some fitting—"

"There is," Ewing said. "Suppose you grant me the freedom of poking around with those notebooks I brought back with me from Earth. All right?"

"Certainly, if that's what you want. But can that be all that—"

"There's just one other thing I want. No, two. The first one may be tough. I want to be left alone. I want to get out of the limelight and stay there. No medals, no public receptions, no more parades. I did the job the Council sent me to do, and now I want to return to private life.

"As for the second thing—well, I won't mention it yet. Let's just put it this way: when the time comes, I'm going to want a favor from the Government. It'll be an expensive favor, but not terribly so. I'll let you know what it is I want, when and if I want it."

Slowly, the notoriety ebbed away, and Ewing returned to private life as he had wished. His life would never be the same again, but there was no help for that. The Council voted him a pension of 10,000 stellors a year, transferable to his heirs in perpetuity, and he was so stunned by their magnanimity that he had no choice but to accept.

A month passed. The tenseness seemed to have left him. He discovered that his son was turning into a miniature replica of his father, tall, taciturn, with the same inner traits of courage, dependability, conscience. It was a startling thing to watch the boy unfolding, becoming a personality.

It was too bad, Ewing thought, as he wrestled with his son or touched his wife's arm, that he would have to be leaving them soon. He would regret parting with them. But at least they would be spared any grief.

A second month passed. The apparatus he was building in his basement, in the sacrosanct den that neither Blade nor Laira ever dared to enter, was nearing completion. The time was drawing near.

He ran the final tests on a warm midsummer day. The machine responded perfectly. The time had come.

He called upstairs via the intercom. Laira was

reading in the study; Blade was watching the video. "Blade? Laira?"

"We're here, Baird. What do you want?" Laira asked.

Ewing said, "I'll be running some very delicate experiments during the next twenty minutes or so. Any shift in the room balance might foul things up. Would you both be kind enough to stay put, in whatever room you're in now, until I give the signal from downstairs?"

"Of course, darling."

Ewing smiled and hung up. Quite carefully he took a massive crowbar from his tool-chest and propped it up at the side of the wall, near the outer door of the den. He glanced at his watch. The time was 1403:30.

He recrossed the room and made some final adjustments on the apparatus. He stared at his watch, letting the minutes go by. Six . . . seven . . . eight . . .

At 1411:30 he reached up and snapped a switch. The machinery hummed briefly and threw him back ten minutes in time.

NINETEEN

HE WAS hovering inches in the air above his own front lawn. He dropped, landing gently, and looked at his watch. The dial said: 1401:30.

At this very moment, he knew, his earlier self was on the house phone, calling upstairs to Laira. Ewing moistened his lips. This would take careful coördination. *Very* careful.

On tiptoe he ran round the house, entering at the side door that led to his basement workshop. He moved stealthily down the inner corridor until he was only a few feet from the workshop door. There, he waited.

There was an intercom outlet mounted in the hall. Gently he lifted the receiver from the hook and put it to his ear.

He heard himself say, "Any shift in the room balance might foul things up. Would you both be kind enough to stay put, in whatever room you're in now, until I give the signal from downstairs?"

"Of course, darling," Laira's voice responded.

Outside, in the hall, Ewing looked at his watch. It read 1403:10. He waited a moment. At 1403:30 he heard the faint *clink* as the crowbar was propped up against the wall near the door.

So far, everything was right on schedule. But here was where he intended to cause a split in the time-track once again.

He edged forward and peered through the partly open door into the workshop. A familiar-looking figure sat with his back to the door, hunched over the time-projector on the table, making fine adjustments preparatory to jumping back in time ten minutes.

His watch said 1405:15.

He stepped quickly into the room and snatched up the crowbar he had so carefully provided for himself. He crossed the room in four quick bounds; his double, absorbed in his work, did not notice until Ewing put his hand on the shoulder of the other and lifted him away from the work bench. In the same motion he swung the crowbar; it smashed into the main section of the time-projector, sending it tumbling to the floor in a tingling crash of breaking tubes and crumbling circuits.

"I hated to do that," he remarked casually. "It represented a lot of work. But *you* know why I did it."

"Y-yes," the other said uncertainly. The two men faced each other over the wreckage of the projector, Baird Ewing facing Baird Ewing, the only difference between them being that one held a crowbar ready for further use. Ewing prayed Laira had not heard the crash. Everything would be ruined if she chose this moment to violate the sanctity of his workroom.

Slowly, he said to his double, "You know who I am and why I'm here, don't you? And where I came from?"

The other ruefully stared down at the wreckage. "I guess so. You got there ahead of me, didn't you? You're one notch up on me in the Absolute time-track."

Ewing nodded. "Exactly. And keep your voice down. I don't want any trouble from you."

"You're determined to do it?"

Ewing nodded again. "Listen to me very carefully, now. I'm going to take my—*our*—car and drive into Broughton. I'm going to make a call to Premier Davidson. Then I'm going to drive out to the spaceport, get into a ship, and leave. That's the last you'll ever hear from me.

"In the meantime, you're to stay down here until at least 1420 or so. Then call upstairs to Laira and tell her you've finished the experiment. Sweep up the wreckage, and if you're a wise man you won't build any more of these gadgets in the future. From now on, no extra Baird Ewings. You'll be the only one. And take good care of Laira and Blade. I love them, too."

"Wait a minute," the other Ewing said. "You're not being fair."

"To whom?"

"To yourself. Look, I'm as much Baird Ewing as you are. And it's as much my responsibility to—to leave Corwin as it is yours. You don't have any right to take it upon yourself to give up everything you love. Let's at least flip a coin to see who goes."

Ewing shook his head. In a quiet, flat voice he said, "No. *I* go. I've watched too many of my alter egos sacrifice themselves to keep me safe and sound."

"So have I, remember?"

Ewing shrugged. "That's tough for you, then. But this is my ride through the time-track, and *I'm* going. You stay here and nurse your guilty conscience, if you like. But you shouldn't moan too much. You'll have Laira and Blade. And Baird Ewing will be doing what he ought to be doing, as well."

"But—"

Ewing lifted the crowbar menacingly. "I don't want to skull you, brother. Accept defeat gracefully."

He looked at his watch. It was 1410. He walked to the door and said, "The car will be parked at the spaceport. You figure out some explanation for how it got there."

He turned and walked out.

The car was waiting in its garage; he touched his finger to the burglar-proof identiplate that controlled the garage door, and the car came out. He got in, switched on the directional guide, and left via the back route, so no one in the house could see him.

As soon as he was comfortably distant from the house, he snapped on the phone circuit and gave the operator Premier Davidson's number.

After a short pause, Davidson acknowledged.

"Hello, Baird. What's on your mind?"

"A favor. You owe me one, remember? I asked for *carte blanche* the day after the Klodni thing."

Davidson chuckled. "I haven't forgotten about it, Baird. Well?"

"I want to borrow a spaceship," Ewing said quietly. "A one-man ship. The same sort of ship I used to get to Earth in, a few years ago."

"A *spaceship?*" The Premier sounded incredulous. "What would you be wanting a spaceship for?"

"That doesn't matter. An experiment of mine, let's say. I asked for a favor, and you said you'd grant it. Are you backing down, now?"

"No, no, of course not. But—"

"Yes. I want a spaceship. I'm on my way to Broughton Spacefield now. Will you phone ahead and tell them to release a military-owned one-man job for me, or won't you?"

It was nearly 1500 when he reached the spacefield. He left his car in the special parking lot and made it on foot across to the trim little building used by the military wing of Corwin's government.

He asked for and was taken to the commanding officer on duty. The officer turned out to be a wry-faced colonel who looked up questioningly as Ewing entered his office.

"You're Ewing, of course."

"That's right. Did Premier Davidson phone?"

The colonel nodded. "He authorized me to give you one of our one-man ships. I guess I don't have to ask if you can operate it, do I?"

Ewing grinned and said, "I guess not."

"The ship's on Field B right now, being serviced for you. It'll be fully fueled, of course. How long are you planning to stay aloft?"

Shrugging, Ewing said, "I really haven't decided

that yet, colonel. But I'll advise for clearance before I come down.''

"Good."

"Oh—one more thing. Is the ship I'm getting equipped for suspension?"

The colonel frowned. ''All our ships are. Why do you ask? Not planning *that* long a trip, are you?''

''Hardly,'' Ewing lied. ''I just wanted to examine the suspension equipment once again. Sentimental reasons, you know.''

The colonel signaled and one of the cadets led him across the field to the waiting ship. It was a twin of the one that had borne him across to Earth; for all he knew, it might have been the very same one. He clambered aboard, switched on the controls, and advised he would be leaving Corwin in eleven minutes.

From memory, he punched out the coördinates for his journey on the autopilot. He activated the unit, stripped, and lowered himself once again into the suspension tank.

He thought:

Firnik thinks I'm dead. He'll be surprised when a ghost turns up on Earth, leading the underground revolt against the Sirians. And I'll have to explain everything very carefully to Myreck as soon as I get back—if I can find Myreck.

And he thought:

My double back home is going to have some fancy explaining to do, too. About what happened to the ship he took up with him, and how his car got to the spaceport while he was in the workship. He'll have

*plenty of fast talking to do. But he'll manage. He's a
pretty shrewd sort. He'll get along.*

He paused for a moment to wish a silent good-bye
to the wife and son who would never know he had left
them. Then he stretched out his feet and switched on
the suspension unit. The temperature began to drop.

Darkness swirled up around him.

TWENTY

THE TIME was 1421, of a warm midsummer afternoon on Corwin. Baird Ewing finished sweeping the shattered fragments of his painstakingly constructed projector into the disposal unit, looked around, put the crowbar back in the tool shelf.

Then he snapped on the housephone and said, "Okay, Laira. The experiment's over. Thanks for helping out."

He hung up and trotted up the stairs to the study. Laira was bent over her book; Blade stared entranced at the video screen. He crept up behind the boy, caught him suddenly with one big hand at the back of his neck, and squeezed affectionately. Then, leaving him, he lifted Laira's head from her viewing screen, smiled warmly at her, and turned away without speaking.

Later in the afternoon he was on his way to Broughton Spacefield via public transport to reclaim his car. He was still some miles distant when the sudden overhead roar of a departing spaceship sounded.

"One of those little military jobs taking off," someone in the bus said.

Ewing looked up through the translucent roof of the bus at the clear sky. No ship was visible, of course. It was well on its way Earthward now.

Good luck, he thought. And Godspeed.

The car was in the special parking field. He smiled to the attendant, unlocked it, climbed in.

He drove home.

Home—to Laira and Blade.

TWENTY

BAIRD EWING woke slowly, sensing the coldness all about him. It was slowly withdrawing down the length of his body; his head and shoulders had come out of the freeze, and the rest of his was gradually emerging.

He looked at the time-panel. Eleven months, fourteen days, six hours had elapsed since he had left Corwin. He hoped they hadn't held their breaths while waiting for him to return their ship.

He performed the de-suspending routine and emerged the tank. He touched the stud and the vision-plate lit up. A planet hung centered in the green depths of the plate—a green planet, with vast seas borderings its continents.

Earth.

Ewing smiled. They would be surprised to see him, all right. But he could help them, and so he had come back. He could serve as coördinator for the resistance movement. He could spearhead the drive that would end the domination of the Sirians.

Here I come, he thought.

His fingers moved rapidly over the manual-control bank of the ship's instrument panel. He began setting up the orbit for landing. Already, plans and counterplans were forming in his active mind.

The ship descended to Earth in a wide-sweeping arc. Ewing waited, impatient for the landing, as his ship swung closer and closer to the lovely green world below.

FRITZ LEIBER

WINNER OF
THE HUGO AWARD
AND THE
NEBULA AWARD
FOR BEST
SCIENCE FICTION
NOVEL OF
THE YEAR

*04594 **Babel 17** Delany $1.50

*05476 **Best Science Fiction of the Year** Del Rey $1.25

06218 **The Big Time** Leiber $1.25

*10623 **City** Simak $1.75

16649 **The Dragon Masters** Vance $1.50

16704 **Dream Master** Zelazny $1.50

19683 **The Einstein Intersection** Delany $1.50

24903 **Four For Tomorrow** Zelazny $1.50

47071 **The Last Castle** Vance 95¢

47803 **Left Hand of Darkness** Leguin $1.95

72784 **Rite of Passage** Panshin $1.50

79173 **Swords and Deviltry** Leiber $1.50

80694 **This Immortal** Zelazny $1.50

Available wherever paperbacks are sold or use this coupon.

━━━━━━━━━━━━━━━━━━━━━━━━━━━━━━

ace books, (Dept. MM) Box 576, Times Square Station
New York, N.Y. 10036
Please send me titles checked above.

I enclose $. . . . . Add 35c handling fee per copy.

Name . . . .

Address . . . .

City. . . . . State . . . . Zip. . . . .

Ursula K. Le Guin

10703	**City of Illusion**	$1.75
47803	**Left Hand of Darkness**	$1.95
66953	**Planet of Exile**	$1.25
73293	**Rocannon's World**	$1.50

Available wherever paperbacks are sold or use this coupon.

★ ★ ★ ★ ★

MARION ZIMMER BRADLEY

20660 **Endless Voyage** $1.25	
31590 **The Halfling** $1.25	

THE DARKOVER SERIES

06852 **Bloody Sun** $1.50	
67020 **Planet Savers** $1.50	
77946 **Star of Danger** $1.50	
79200 **Sword of Aldones** $1.50	

Available wherever paperbacks are sold or use this coupon.

ace books, (Dept. MM) Box 576, Times Square Station
New York. N.Y. 10036
Please send me titles checked above.
I enclose $. . . . . Add 35c handling fee per copy.

Name . . . .

Address . . . .

City. . . . . State. . . . . Zip. . . . .

70 A